Rainmaker

Rainmaker

by
Don Pinnock

JACANA

First printed by Jacana Media (Pty) Ltd in 2010

10 Orange Street
Sunnyside
Auckland Park 2092
South Africa
+2711 628 3200
www.jacana.co.za

ISBN 978-1-77009-780-3

The chapter images are tracings of /Xam rock art and were made by **Siyakha Mguni** of Bushman's Kloof, who are custodians of beautiful natural rock galleries in the Cederberg, South Africa

Cover design by banana republic
Set in Sabon 11/14pt
Job No 001062
Printed and bound by CTP Printers, Cape Town
ISO 12647 compliant

See a complete list of Jacana titles at www.jacana.co.za

I am the land of early times
I am the time of the blackest night
I am the sound of the distant rain
I am the spring that never dies
I am the scent of the *shoo-/oa* root
I am a star in the waterpit
I am */xue* who is all things
I am the dying moon. Who but I
Walks the sky at dusk?

I am the wings of the dreaming Mantis
I am the song of the beast of prey
I am the tobacco pouch stolen by a dog
I am a stripe on the springbuck's side
I am the horn on the antelope's head
I am the dancing rattle of springbuck ears
I am the spoor of the eland
I am the waterhole. Who but I
Passes from father to son?

From *Claim to the Country*
by Pippa Skotnes

In memory of the /Xam people
and the shamans of rain

A guide to /Xam click symbols

/ the sound made when the tip of the tongue is pressed against the front teeth and quickly withdrawn.

! the sound when the tongue is pressed against the roof of your mouth and released sharply downwards, like when a cork is pulled from a bottle.

// the sound produced at the side of your tongue when your tongue is pressed against the roof of your mouth and air is sucked in, like a sound of annoyance.

I should start where the trouble began, here in Bonteheuwel with all its sand and dust. I was a member of the Blood Brothers gang and we were going to war. There are always reasons for war. This one was because the Tough Livings had killed a cousin of Cliffie's named Kajuit in the Athlone Lounge. They came up behind him as he walked out of the toilet and stabbed him with two long knives down through his shoulder blades and into his heart. They did this because Kajuit's brother had shot a Tough Livings who had come into the Blood Brothers' territory. These things go back to where you can't remember and nobody seems able to stop the revenge stuff.

It all begins when you sit round with your brothers and you've got nothing to do but smoke white pipe. Someone remembers this incident and someone else remembers that insult and eventually a soldier says: 'We're going to nail those bastards.' Then you get excited and high and talk about the battle you're planning.

That day, when all this started, we thought we had a really smart plan. We'd pretend to be Tough Livings coming from another area so we could get close to their headquarters, then let all hell loose. Thursday morning – I remember it was

Thursday because that's the day my Ma doesn't work – we headed out of our territory with guns stuck in our belts under our shirts.

We got to the Tough Livings' headquarters without being seen. 'We're TLs,' I shouted, giving the two fingers and thumb blood sign of the prison gang that's linked to the Tough Livings. Norman closed up behind me and I remember hearing the *click-click* as he pulled back the slider of the nine-mill pistol. The lookout stepped out of the doorway grinning, then saw us and tried to slam it shut. Norman's gun went *badoom* behind my head, making my ears ring, and the round went right through the wood before the guy could close the door. He was inside, screaming. Chicken and Cliffie ran round the wrecked bakkie they'd been hiding behind and Norman blasted another round into the opening to make sure nobody tried to defend it.

He ran up and smashed a bathroom window with his gun and looked inside, in case someone was covering the front door from there. A woman was on the toilet and she shrieked high-pitched, like women do. Then Norman leapt inside, his guns going *badoom*, *badoom*. I jumped after him and fired at the television screen. It gave a loud *pouf* and the voice coming out of it hung in the air for a bit. Then everything went quiet. There was nobody in the room.

'We're Blood Brothers,' Norman yelled, making me jump. 'You're shit! You're just Tough Living shit! Come out or I'll blast you out! You're going to die for killing Kajuit.'

'It's you who's going to die,' said an awful voice, big and deep and not afraid. I can still hear it. The door of the bedroom opened slowly like there was no hurry here.

'Christ! It's Akker,' Chicken said softly, as though he didn't want anyone to hear. Akker stepped into the lounge, not interested in the guns we were pointing at him. He was dressed all neat, creased trousers, silk shirt, gold dollar-sign cufflinks. It was like a movie. His eyes dug into me.

I need to explain about Akker. He and his brother controlled all the Tough Livings on the Cape Flats, not just in Bonteheuwel. He was bad news. They called him The Lion because he ripped people to pieces who got in his way. He was related to Mikey Ismael who was a member of the Globe Gang in District Six long ago, before the government tore it down. They all lived in Meul Street. Akker shot his way to the top of gangland. When he was leader of the City Scorpions, they took over the territory of the Skunky Kids by surrounding their shebeen and throwing in pipe bombs filled with nails. They killed everyone inside. People still talk about that even though it was back in the 1980s. Then he and his brother formed the Tough Livings. They grabbed most of the Mandrax market, then the crack market in the 90s.

Akker was clever. He used to go into public places with arms full of money and throw it up so the people could catch it. People loved him for that and they never ratted on him. He started mobile shops that sold food out the front and drugs out the back. He bribed policemen. He bribed *captains* of the police. He killed many people but he never went to court. Akker was untouchable – and just about the worst person to meet in a room you'd just shot up.

'You brown trash,' he said slow-like. 'You come into my sister's house and shoot at people. You think this is a television programme, hey? You think because you have a little pea-shooter you can rule the Cape Flats? Is that what you think? Hey?'

'I didn't know you were…' I started to say.

'You think you can smash my sister's bathroom window and point a gun at her when she's pregnant?' He just went on talking like I'd said nothing. 'You're a *niks*, you're just brown trash, the son of a *Boesman* mother. You have a little bow and arrow and you think you can come and fight with me?'

That made me go mad. Really crazy mad. The anger just

came up inside me. These days that anger is strange for me. But '*Boesman*' was a bad thing to say. It made my throat want to close. It was something people had teased me about all my life because of how I looked.

'*Boesman*?' I said. 'You call me a *Boesman*? You think I'm a *Hotnot*?' My voice was funny and high. My gun just went *bang*. I don't remember pulling the trigger. Akker clutched his leg and rolled onto the couch, which tipped over. It crashed into the chairs and they all slammed into the dining room table.

'You mad?' Norman screamed at me. 'You bloody mad?' He jumped towards the door, crashing Chicken into the frame. Then he started to run. I was standing there just staring at the mess and at Akker getting up and the TV in pieces all over the carpet. Then I realised my brothers were gone so I beat the hell out of the door. We ran up the road. Cliffie was shouting questions. He had been standing watch outside. 'What went wrong? Why are you running?'

'This prick shot Akker,' Norman yelled. 'He bloody shot him.'

'Oh God! Oh no,' Cliffie made a strange noise in his throat. 'You're a dead man, Ky. You're dead, man.'

I was listening to my Nikes *slap-slapping* the cement road. My chest hurt from the running and I was hanging onto my gun to stop it hammering my hip. My head was *deurmekaar*.

'I didn't kill him,' I shouted as the guys dived round a corner to get out of possible line of fire from the headquarters. 'I just hit him in the leg.'

You're gonna wish you *had* killed him,' Norman shouted at me. 'Because now he'll have your name on every bullet in every Tough Living's gun. That makes a lot of bullets coming your way.'

'Nobody calls me a bloody *Boesman*. Nobody. Akker asked for it. And this isn't a bow and arrow. It's a nine-mill.'

'Akker can call you what he likes, bro,' said Chicken, puffing like crazy in those silly leather shoes he likes. 'He's got the biggest outfit in the Cape. He can call on two thousand guns if he needs to and, shit, he will. We're all on the list now.'

I said: '*Ag*, shut up. You're just using up air!' But I was getting really scared.

The big Blood Brothers' flag and eagle mural on Uitsig flats was up ahead – the beginning of our territory. Just past it, we slowed down and began ducking through the courtyards. The southeaster was kicking up stinging sand and making washing on the lines between the buildings roar and flap. Then we came to the big, red BBs – that's our sign, Blood Brothers.

'God, that Tough Living rolled through the door.' Norman was boasting like he always does.

'Yeah, but he wasn't in the room so you couldn't have nailed him proper, bro,' Chicken teased.

'He probably ran to help his mommy with her tummy,' said Norman.

'You think it's funny?' I was freaked. 'What the hell am I gonna do now?'

'Dig a hole and stay there for a year,' said Cliffie. He looked completely serious. 'I mean it – you must vanish or you've had it. He got a good look at you – he won't forget who you are. We're in trouble, but the stuff's right over your head.'

'So? Suggestions, wise guy.'

'I dunno,' said Norman. 'The Cape Flats has too many eyes. People will sell you for a few *kroon*.'

'But I don't know anywhere else.' I was starting to look over my shoulder like Akker was limping after me already. 'I'd stick out like a *skollie* anywhere else.'

'We'd better disappear,' said Chicken. 'Akker's surely getting a hunting party together while he bleeds. Hey, brothers, this is serious *kak* we're in. I didn't know that was his sister's place.

I'll talk to Stone, but I don't think he'll want a war over this. Find somewhere safe, Ky, and I'll see you at the burnt-out bus at ten tonight. If I'm not there, just keep low till the next night same time.'

My mind was spinning. Even now, when I remember, I get cold shivers. Every open area felt like the place for a clear shot at my back. I ran across to Bellview Flats then along them until I reached Dysan Court.

'Hey, Ma.' I burst through the door. 'I'm in trouble. There was a problem. Someone hassled me and I got angry and shot him in the leg. He's okay but...'

'No, Ky! What are you doing with a gun? Why do you move with those rubbish friends?' she shouted at me. She can be really stupid sometimes. Who else can I be friends with?

'Aaai! I wish you had a father around. Who was it?'

'Akker.'

'*Akker*?'

I nodded.

'Oh Jesus, no! *Ag nee* Ky. It can't be. How *could* you? He's... he's so dangerous. Ky, oh Ky, he's, he's.... You shouldn't have done that.'

I was really shocked to see how she was going on. It made me more scared. Tears were smudging her face.

'Don't worry, Ma,' I said. 'It's just I must hide. It will blow over.' I held her by the shoulders. She was crying so much, like she was choking. These days I know why, but not then.

'You have to go. Now,' she said. 'You must go very quickly. They will come here first.'

'But they don't even know you, Ma,' I told her. 'Why should they come here?'

'They know you are my son. They'll come here first. You have to go,' she begged.

'How come they know?' I said.

'Akker... we've known each other for ages. He'll come here. He will. I'm telling you. Go, go, go.' She pushed me out the door. 'Go hide somewhere, please Ky, don't stay here. It will be terrible.'

Hey, I just backed away from her and down the stairs. My own Ma had pushed me out when I needed her most. Where could I go? I turned round and tried to walk normally, but the flats seemed to have guns pointing out of every window. I found a place under a stairwell and sat in its shadow – suddenly, like all the air went out of me. It was crazy to go walking around in daylight. I sat there for hours, listening to my heartbeat, wondering what to do, until it was dark. I crept out to the burnt bus at ten but Norman wasn't there and I couldn't hang around. Had they got him? I needed a safe place to hide. Then I thought of a plan. But it was shaky.

I knew a girl from school called Auri. She was very smart, straight As and all that. We'd made friends after she'd let me copy some of her maths homework. We spent quite a bit of time together at school and talked a lot about stuff. I'd walked home with her after class a few times, but we weren't out-of-school friends. I guess she didn't like my gang connections. Right then, I couldn't think of anyone else safe to ask for help – and she lived nearby. Staying in the shadows I walked to where she lived and tapped on her window.

'Hey, Auri, let me in, quick.'

The side of the flats was high and black above me. The

toilet pipes made V-patterns on their way down into the sand. A window above was flickering blue from a TV and I remember the sound of radio adverts coming from somewhere else. When you're scared, things like that stick in your mind. I ducked behind a corrugated iron fence as a car's lights swept across. Then I tapped again.

'Auri!'

The lace curtain opened and she looked out.

'Who is it? What you want?' She sounded sleepy.

'It's Ky. You got to let me in, I'm in trouble,' I said, trying to whisper and be loud enough for her to hear.

'It's late. I can't just let you in. My parents are asleep. Go away.'

'Please, this is serious. You're the only one I know who can help me.'

Auri opened the window and looked out. I didn't wait. I climbed on a pipe and swung onto the sill and into her room. It was tiny, with only a bed, a desk and a cupboard. Tick-tacked onto the wall was a poster of a mountain with elephants below it. The room smelled like a girl.

She put a gown over her pyjamas and sat down next to me looking a bit cross but her eyes were smiling. You know how girls can do that?

'What's so important that you should come and wake me up in the middle of the night?'

'I shot Akker.'

'You whaaat?'

'I didn't kill him. It was a mistake. We didn't know he was there. I dunno why I shot him. He called me a *Boesman*.'

'You shot him because he called you a *Boesman*? You're crazy, Ky. Why do you hang out with those Blood Brother *skollies*? You know what's going to happen to you if he finds you?'

'I know,' I said, looking at my shoes. 'I thought you may

be able to hide me. Nobody would think to look for me here. Your family's so respectable.'

'But, so what must I do? I can't just stick you under my bed. You can't fit in my wardrobe. My mom comes in here, my Pa. Anyway, it's just not right, you in my room in the night like this.'

'I'll be dead if I go out,' I said. 'I can't go to my Ma's house. If I go to my uncle's place he'd probably *take* me to Akker. You know how it is with him and me. My friends won't go near me when they know Akker's got a finger on me.'

'Some friends!' Auri said. 'So now you come here and think it's okay for me if Akker finds you here?'

'I'm sorry, Auri,' I told her. 'I didn't know where else to go. You always seemed to know what to do. You're so cool. I just thought....'

'Look, I've got to wake up my Pa.

'No!'

'I have to. You can't spend the night here in my room! We're not... no I have to get him. Wait here.'

She slipped out and I got ready to dive out the window in case her Pa came in with a gun or something. There was shuffling outside the door and a light was switched on. It was so bright! When Mr Kabbo stepped in, I can tell you, I *skrikked*. He's short, like Auri, but he looked big standing there in his gown and I think it must have been his wife's pompom slippers. He had a wrinkled face and fierce eyes. I didn't jump out the window. I just collapsed on the desk stool like my legs had stopped working.

'So you're in trouble and you come through my daughter's window?' he said in a soft, growly voice. Then he did something strange. He grinned and sat down on the bed. 'Gang stuff, hey Ky? When are you going to learn that gangs are just trouble? They don't give you what you're looking for. Perhaps you'd better tell me the story, and then we can find some blankets.

You can use the couch, but you'll have to leave tomorrow. This is a small place.'

I tell you I could have cried, right there on the stool. I just told him there was a war going on between gangs and I was in trouble because I'd wounded Akker. I didn't want to say any more. He shook his head, kind of sadly.

I was soon asleep on the couch like I'd also been shot. It felt so safe. That's when I had the first dream.

In the heat of sun I hear only the gurgling of the river as I bend to drink. I've been stalking an eland I shot earlier in the morning and it led me over the mountains and through some valleys. This was a strong animal and it didn't seem to be getting tired from the poison.

A huff of something breathing out makes me spin around. It's too late. The lion is only one leap away and moving at terrible speed. I jump forward but the lion's teeth sink into my shoulder and I fall under its weight. It lets go for a moment and I'm surprised that I feel no pain. Then the lion drags me away from the river towards a bent, old cedar tree. I struggle but the lion bites me harder, so I go limp. My only hope is to play dead and hope it lets me go long enough to escape.

It drops me next to the tree and takes a few steps back towards the river. I watch him through slitted eyes and just lie there, pretending to be dead. The lion must be thirsty because it stalks down to drink. The pain from the bite suddenly becomes bad. I nearly cry out, but I force myself to lie still by squeezing my eyes shut. Tears come out and run down the side of my face. Perhaps the lion sees this because it runs back to me. It sniffs my eyes and I feel its tongue like sandpaper scraping the side of my face, licking the tears. I lie still. I'm terrified. It must decide I'm really dead because it walks into the trees by the bank. As it disappears, I drag myself to my feet and begin to run. Gradually, I run faster. I go as quietly as a hunter along a valley I know will take me down the Chameleon Mountains and to my people.

I jerked awake, panting like I'd been running for real. What a weird dream! My shoulder was sore. I must have been sleeping on it. I didn't know where I was or why I was lying down. I was supposed to be escaping from the lion. Then I remembered. And I can tell you it was better to be escaping from a lion than from Akker. The room was dark and the only sound was the ticking of a clock and the wail of a siren outside.

I was in someone else's home and in deep trouble. I tried to go back to sleep but couldn't. Where could I go? I couldn't hide in the flat. Mr Kabbo had said so. This meant I'd have to leave at first light while an army was prowling the streets for me. I lay there staring at the ceiling, hoping the sun wouldn't rise. But it did.

'Hey, Ky!' It was Auri. 'I've got to go to school. What are you going to do?'

I sat up and groaned: 'Aargh, what a night.'

'Sure, you gave me quite a night too. Didn't you sleep?'

'Ja, I did,' I told her, 'and dreamed about being attacked by a lion. It bit me and licked my tears, but I got away.'

Auri looked at me strangely, then yanked the blanket away.

'Up! Let's have some breakfast.'

I sat at the kitchen table while Auri stirred some oats. She was so pretty, moving about like that, her heart-shaped face with a look that seemed to be always at the edge of laughter. She scooped porridge into two plates, fetched the milk and sat opposite me.

'Morning,' Mr Kabbo said, walking into the kitchen. 'Sleep okay on the couch, Ky?'

'Yes, sir,' I said.

'So what are your plans?'

'I don't know. I have to stay out of sight or I'm going to be in big trouble.'

'Akker is a mean character and he's got a big gang. Couldn't you have picked on someone less dangerous?' he asked and helped himself to some porridge.

'Well, sir, he said I was a *niks*. He called me brown trash and said I was a little *Boesman* with a bow and arrow. I just got angry and pulled the trigger.'

'What's wrong with being a Bushman?' he asked.

'Well, I mean, he shouldn't insult me like that,' I replied.

'Right, well, Ky you must leave as soon as you're finished eating,' he said. 'I hope you've got somewhere to go.'

'Yes, sir. I mean, no sir, I haven't got anywhere to go. Could I…?'

'No, Ky,' he replied. 'I'm not prepared to put Auri and her mother at risk because of what you did. I don't approve of you carrying a gun. I don't like gangs. No, you can't stay here.'

'Okay.'

'Well, at least the lion didn't catch you in your dream,' Auri said. I guess she was trying to break the awkwardness in the room. 'So I'm sure that's a good sign for you.'

'What lion?' asked Mr Kabbo.

'Ky had a dream about being bitten by a lion. It licked his tears, but he got away,' said Auri.'

'Tell me the dream, boy,' Mr Kabbo said. He seemed fierce, like I'd said something wrong.

I mumbled: 'Oh, it was just a dream.'

But he said: 'No, don't get vague. Tell me.' So I did, though it seemed a bit silly at the time, telling a stranger my dream like that. He stopped me every now and then and asked questions.

'How were you dressed?'

'I don't remember. I don't think I had many clothes on. I remember looking at where the lion was biting me and there were no clothes on my shoulder.'

Then he asked: 'How did you know it was a cedar tree?'

'I don't know. It just was.'

'Have you ever seen a cedar tree?'

'No, sir.'

'What did the tops of the mountains look like? Were they very jagged?'

'Yes. I remember knowing they were called the Chameleon Mountains.'

'Hah!' he said, slapping his hand on the table. 'Chameleon Mountains!'

Auri looked startled. Her father didn't often get excited about things.

'What's going on?' called Auri's mother from the bedroom. 'You okay, Hin?'

'I'm fine,' Mr Kabbo said. 'Look, Ky, don't go out of the house. Don't look out of the windows. Just sleep or something, but don't show yourself. I'm going to talk to a friend and we'll see about things when I come home.'

Hey, I just looked at him with my mouth open. So did Auri.

'You mean I can…?'

'Just stay away from the windows and don't go outside,' he said again. 'I'm late for work. Auri, school time. Hurry up now.'

The turnaround really muddled me, but I can tell you I was glad I didn't have to be out in broad daylight. While I helped Mrs Kabbo clean the kitchen, I kept imagining hundreds of gangsters, armed with nine-mills, poking round the township for me. Did they have orders to kill me, or just shoot my legs so Akker could kill me slowly later? Every time I heard a car outside I waited for the bang on the door or the smash of a window. It was a bad day and it went by slowly. Eventually I crashed on the couch and fell asleep.

'Wake up, Ky.' Mr Kabbo's voice broke into my dreams and jerked me awake. 'This is Pieter Kwi.'

'I was sleeping,' I mumbled, embarrassed that the two men had to wake me up. They could have been Akker and I hadn't been watching.

'It's a good thing, sleep,' said Mr Kabbo and sat down. 'Would you mind telling Pieter your dream about the lion?'

'My dream?'

'Yes.'

'But why?

'For the moment, never mind why,' he said. 'Just know that your life might depend on it right now.'

So I told his friend the dream. From time to time Pieter nodded and went, 'Hmm, yes'. When I was finished Mr Kabbo asked him: 'Is it one?'

'Yes, it is. It's just the beginning. It may not go further. But it's one of the First Dreams.'

I didn't know what they were talking about.

'Look, Ky,' Mr Kabbo said, 'we can get you out of town tonight. At my work people were talking about the shooting.'

I felt a cold shiver.

'You have to make a choice,' Mr Kabbo went on. 'Where

we would take you is far from Cape Town. It's a pretty wild place, but you'll be safe with a friend called Zimry. We'll tell your mother you're okay but we can't let anyone know where you'll be. Will you manage that?'

This all sounded strange and I wasn't sure what he meant by a wild place. Then I thought about all those guns looking for me just outside the door and nowhere could be wilder than that.

'Yes, I have to go,' I said. 'I can't stay in Cape Town, so I'll go. But why are you doing this for me?'

'Never mind why,' Pieter told me again. 'If you're prepared to go we'll help you. It may be very tough in the mountains. You'll have to be strong. And Zimry takes no nonsense.'

'What mountains?' I asked. I guess I expected a small village somewhere.

'Perhaps we should call them the Chameleon Mountains,' said Mr Kabbo with a grin.

I wondered if they were making fun of my dream. I asked, 'Who's Zimry?'

'He'll tell you himself,' Pieter replied. His answer didn't make me keen to meet him.

That evening they fetched me. Mr Kabbo gave me an old coat and jersey and made me pull a balaclava over my face. I was scared of going out. The streets were dark except for those sputnik lights down near Main Road. I got in the back of Mr Kabbo's car – it was an old Cortina with a red stripe down the side. Pieter was in the passenger seat and he made me lie down and put a blanket over me. It smelled of smoke. Then they drove and drove. When I asked them where they were going, I had to shout because the engine was making such a noise. They laughed and Pieter said, 'Chameleon Mountains, remember?' That didn't put me in a good mood. I mean, when you're under a blanket in a car going to a place in a dream, and they're just teasing you and talking rubbish.... *Juss*, I was mad. But even more, I was scared, so I didn't get up and look.

We drove forever. Every now and then I would hear a car *whoosh* past, but even they stopped passing eventually and I looked out. There was nothing much to see. So I went to sleep and woke up when the car got onto a dirt road and began to bump and sway. It was black, black out there, with only the headlights picking up bushes on the side of the road. Once I saw a rabbit in the road. It froze for a moment before running ahead of us and finally escaped into the grass.

I could see the shape of huge mountains, dark against the stars. We stopped at a gate and Pieter opened it. But we didn't ride from there. Mr Kabbo parked under a tree and we got out.

'From here you and Pieter must walk. I'll wait with the car,' said Mr Kabbo. He shook my hand. 'Tell Zimry your dream. That is important. Tell him I will see him here in a month's time.'

'Am I going to be here for a month?' I asked.

'How long do you think Akker's memory is?' he said. That made me feel really down. With all the other stuff going on, I hadn't thought about when I would be able to stop hiding. I was also confused about why these men were helping me.

Pieter was a fast walker. It was dark and steep and I was panting. It was a good thing there was a moon, because there wasn't a clear path. I followed Pieter over the grass, round low bushes and rocks. Hey, we walked! It wasn't nice. I didn't know where we were going. I thought maybe it was just a little way from the car but we climbed for hours. Pieter just didn't get tired. We were lucky there were streams to drink from or I would have died on the spot. We seemed to go right over the mountains. I looked back when it began to get light and could see the land far away below and dams and a road like a piece of string with the sky all pink.

The mountains were like monsters. Really, I mean they had monsters' heads on them. The rocks were twisted and some had holes right through them. I'd never climbed a mountain before. Ja, you laugh. But where do you see a mountain in a township?

When we went over the top, the sight made me just want to sit right there, or maybe go back home and deal with Akker. It wasn't too far down – well, not very far – but all I could see from there were mountains and more mountains and valleys. And there was this huge, black eagle flying nearby, Pieter told me what it was. I'd never seen a real eagle before, only the Blood Brothers mural on our wall. All that *nothing* was really, really scary. And the morning sky seemed to go on forever.

Pieter was in a hurry, that's for sure. He just kept going and I had to follow. Nearly at the bottom of the valley I saw a hut and I thought, 'Oh no, not there.' But we carried on right down to it. There was a man sitting outside on a rock watching us but he was so still I thought he was part of the rock and got a fright when he moved. He was dressed in khaki shorts and a khaki shirt and had tags on his shoulders like a policeman. He stood up as we arrived, put one hand on his heart, then held it forwards. Pieter did the same and they touched palms.

'Good morning,' he said. 'A long walk, hey? I'm Zimry. Who are you?'

I said, 'Ky Rahl,' but my mind was in a knot because his name meant this rotten little hut was where I was going to hide. It was made of flat stones all piled on top of each other with cement in-between and a grass roof. It had an ordinary door and windows but there was nothing else and nobody else for I don't know how far. When I looked at the hut I realised it was built just outside a big cave, which was open like the mouth of a snoek.

'You like my house?' Zimry asked. I don't remember what I answered. He looked like an old man with his face all wrinkled like a screwed-up *lap* and he had little *peperkorreltjies* of hair all over his head like a Bushman. He and Pieter talked for a bit then Pieter nodded in my direction and said: 'Ky had one of the dreams. Kabbo wants you to see if he has the Gift.' That's all. Then he set off the way we'd come.

I was really spooked. There I was in the middle of nowhere with this funny little man, Zimry. He offered me some *rooibos*. I was pretty thirsty and it tasted nice, but I didn't know what to say.

'He knows nothing about me,' I thought. 'He doesn't even ask any questions. He doesn't seem to be interested.'

I finished drinking and I wasn't sure what to do next. I mean, what do you do when there's nothing to do? I asked Zimry where I could sleep, and hoped he wouldn't point at the cave. He took me inside the hut and showed me a corner with a mat and some blankets. No mattress, no pillow. That sort of did it for me. I said 'Oh, *nooit*' and went off and sat near the cave, really freaked out. How the hell had I got myself into this? I mean, there were no shops! Nothing. I couldn't even run away. I didn't know where I was. I sat thinking about Norman and Chicken and Ma and ended up crying like a snot-nose. Maybe Zimry saw. I don't know. I didn't care. When I looked, he had gone. I didn't know what to do so I lay down in the shade and went to sleep. When I woke up the sun was setting. I looked in the hut but Zimry wasn't inside. He wasn't in the cave either. Hey, it gave me a big fright. A bit earlier I was wishing I'd never met him. Now I was uptight because he'd disappeared. I shouted 'Zimry!' but there was no answer.

I searched for him everywhere, feeling sorry for myself. After a while, Zimry's voice said: 'There is a time to shout in these mountains but sunset is not that time.'

I jumped sky high. He was standing right behind me with some wood on his shoulder.

'I was collecting. It'll be cold tonight. The air's still and last night there was a circle round the moon.'

Zimry made some stew for us. He threw in some bits of meat and chopped vegetables I'd never seen before. Then he added dry herbs from a branch that was hanging in the hut. All the while he was humming under his breath. The food tasted delicious and I was hungry. When I asked him what meat it was he said that it was dassie. I nearly threw up. He'd caught it the day before. Then he pointed to the vegetables on his plate and said he'd picked them on the way up from the river.

Over supper I told Zimry what Kabbo had said and then I told him my dream. He nodded all the time. When I was finished he said, 'Kabbo was right to send you.' I didn't tell him about Akker. It was none of his business.

That night I slept badly. It was so quiet all I could hear was my heart beating. I was used to voices from the shebeen across the road and cars and sirens. There was always a radio going somewhere. I'd never slept on a mat and had to use Mr Kabbo's coat as a pillow so I got cold. When I lay still for a while, bits of my body hurt. And the more they hurt, the angrier I got about being in this place. Then when I was really sleepy Zimry started snoring. By the time it became light, I was in a bad mood. Zimry was outside making the fire. Breakfast was warmed-up dassie and I ate it.

I don't know how I got through that day. Zimry was doing all sorts of things that made no sense to me and I just felt bad. I wanted to be anywhere but in those scary mountains. If I was going to be there for a month – I couldn't think about being there longer – I was going to be bored out of my mind. No TV, nothing but clouds and this old man. And boiled dassie.

I think I sulked for a week. Zimry just did his own thing and left me alone. Because he and the clouds were the only things moving I started to watch him. Each morning at sunrise he took water in a cup and threw it in a sparkling curve towards the sun. Then he took some feathers – I'd never seen such huge feathers before – and stuck them upright in poles that I later discovered were north, south, east and west of the hut. After that he went into the cave and sat for a long time before he walked down to the stream and washed his body by first rubbing it with mud he made from the river sand. Then he jumped into a deep pool, disappearing into the water. When he came up he was clean. But the water was so cold. I thought: 'If I do that, I'll die.' Anyway, I couldn't swim. He also made squares on the ground with pegs and white tape. When I asked him what they were for he said: 'For counting'. It didn't make any sense.

Apart from tea and a bag of flour and some sugar, there was no food in the hut. Zimry never seemed to hunt – you know, with spears and things – but he would go for a walk and pick up food on the way. He ate everything – all sorts of vegetables and even insects. One day he came back with a bag of scorpions. He shook them out into a box, then cut off their tails and threw them in a pot of boiling water. When they were cooked he crushed them all into a mush with flour and made fire bread with it. He scraped the fire to one side and buried the dough in sand and pushed the coals back over the top. Later, he dug out the bread and dusted off the sand. I couldn't eat it right then. But the next morning I was hungry and tried some. It was okay and wasn't even sandy. Then one day we had rice. I was surprised. It was a bit oily but tasted great. I said to him: 'Wow, this is really cool rice.'

He said: 'Ja, it's Bushman rice. Termites.'

I spat them out. 'What do you mean "termites"?'

'The things you find in those mounds.'

'I'm eating *ants*?'

'No, termite eggs. Ants are flightless wasps. Termites are from the cockroach family.'

'Sis! I *am* eating ants!' I just sat there staring at my plate. Zimry didn't say anything, he just went on munching. Then he sighed, took my plate and ate mine too.

Mostly, Zimry didn't really talk. He said necessary things or asked if I wanted another helping or some tea. It wasn't conversation. But he seemed to be watching me, looking for something. It was driving me crazy. I was starting to talk to the lizards that sat on the rocks outside the cave. Then, one day, just to make some sort of talk, I asked:

'How do you catch dassies so easily?'

'I'll show you,' he said, and went on cutting away at a stick with his pocket knife. I thought it was probably easier to talk to his stick. Next morning, after I got up still feeling sore from sleeping on the floor, Zimry said 'Come' and walked off. I didn't know where he was going. He walked so fast I almost had to run to keep up. This old man, I thought, he just doesn't add up. And we *walked*. All morning. Through a wild valley with these huge mountains high up on each side. Every now and then a buck, which I later learned was a duiker, would spring up and bounce away. It always made me jump, my heart hammering.

'I really need to stop,' I pleaded.

'Okay, we can wait by this stream,' he said. I was exhausted. Zimry dug up some roots.

'Here, try these. Good for energy.' They tasted okay. But soon we were off again. We went along a flat area for a bit, then climbed another steep slope that wasn't so high but really bushy and hard to get up. From the top I could see farmlands and a house in the valley far below. I thought maybe I should run to the farm and ask if I could stay there. But the farmer would probably hand me to the police for trespassing. So I forgot that idea. Right at the edge of a cliff Zimry, who was ahead of me, just disappeared. I got a fright and ran forward. Then his voice came out of the rocks almost under my feet. I jumped back and nearly fell. He said: 'Be careful and come down the hole just to your right.' Sure enough, there was a hole. It was like a chimney going down and I was afraid of getting stuck. But Zimry just hopped down further and I wasn't going to let him think I was scared or anything. So I climbed down after him. The hole wasn't deep and I dropped into the back of a cave in the cliff face. The view from up there was forever. You could see right across the valley and the mountains beyond.

Zimry was looking the other way, at the wall. I really thought he was mad. Then I looked at the wall too. He was staring at three tiny paintings of a man holding a spear and throwing a club at a little buck. Just behind the man, who was about the size of my thumb, was a bigger buck. They were beautiful. I couldn't stop looking at them. I could almost feel the club in my hand and I knew where it was going to hit the creature right behind its front legs. I got a funny feeling all over my body and I felt myself falling into the painting. Like falling, but not moving. I stepped back from the wall and Zimry grabbed my arm because I'd nearly gone out of the cave backwards. That would have been a long fall. He was looking at me with his eyebrows way up and a big smile. I didn't think it was funny. I'd nearly killed myself.

'This is Hunter's Cave,' he told me. 'Sit down and I'll begin the story of hunting. It's long because it's also the story of life and death. I have to begin with where we came from.' Zimry was *talking!* He spoke for a long time and I hadn't yet learned how to hear with my heart. So there's probably a lot that I've forgotten.

This is a story about the Beginning, but also about the Other Side. In the first dark underworld there was nothing. Then the First Being of the Early Race who we call !khwe took the sun out from under his armpit and threw it up. Everything began.

His breath made nine Early Race people who were also stars. And six ants and three beetles who were people too. There were no stones or any trees or grass or green things.

At each of the four directions – north, south, east and west – was a round hut with four rooms one above the other. There the Watchers of All Directions lived. All these people spoke the same language, the language of /Xam-ka!au. Today, wild animals still understand it. Chief among these Watchers was Mantis, who is called in our language /Kaggen.

After discussion, the Watchers built a house at the centre with four rooms, one above each other. In it, /Kaggen dreamed the shape of what was to come. All the people went into the first room. Then they climbed into the second. There were still no stones or trees and it was dark. There they met some Locust People and they all went into the third chamber. It was a place without limits but not good to live in and filled with dangerous star-fires. It was flickering with dots and zigzags and spirals. A locust said they should go up further, but the others didn't trust the Locust People. So they discussed among themselves. But eventually they did go up. There they met First Man, First Woman and Jackal. Also //Khai-hemm, who is the bush fire that eats all things. It was the beginning of our world that /Kaggen had dreamed.

First Man had treasures: Red Ochre, Blue Agate, Black Sky Stone, Clear Water Stone and Gold Sun Stone. These he put in the north, south, east, west with the Water Stone in the centre. Then he breathed on them. Five cloud columns rose and met overhead and day and night were born. /Kaggen went to each stone and took into himself their colours. The Water Stone he put against his heart and took some of its brightness. This way his power increased. He became the chief Keeper of All Directions.

All the people and creatures lived in the fourth chamber for a year but became restless. Then /Kaggen said they should all hold onto the middle cloud column which was like a shining thread. It pulled them into the Red World. As they went, First Man rolled up his cloud columns and tucked them into his belt. He also took his stones.

In the Red World, /Kaggen made Eland. He loved his eland but it was stolen by the meerkats and eaten. /Kaggen was angry because eland was his messenger, but he forgave the meerkats and made many eland. This was so people would remember the Red-World spirit. /Kaggen took a small water stone from his treasure and gave it to the eland so they would not get thirsty.

In the Red World were also Moth People. /Kaggen blew on the Moth People so they'd find air. There he met Dassie and married her.

Zimry stopped talking. It was a really strange story. And it didn't make any sense. I thought: 'Hey, this guy is crazier than I imagined.'

'How's that going to help me hunt dassies?' I asked, 'And why did you bring me all this way to tell me that story?'

'This is Hunter's Cave,' he said again. 'It's here you get the power of hunting. But first you must know who it is you hunt. You can't kill things without knowing who they are. You must know their names in their language, /Xam-ka!au. Otherwise they won't come to you and you may not take their lives. Dassie is a creature of the Red World and its name is */hun*.' He said the name with a click in front, like 'ts' and told me to say it. It wasn't easy to say 'ts' and 'hun' together. My tongue didn't want to work that way.

'Practise,' Zimry told me. He got up and climbed out of the cave and I followed. When I caught up he was carrying a dassie. He'd just grabbed it right there as he climbed out of the cave. He cut open its stomach with his pocket knife and pulled out the guts. All that blood and pink stuff looked horrible. Then he skinned it like peeling a banana, cut off bits and laid them on a rock. We made a fire and cooked it by holding the meat over the flames on sticks. It popped and sizzled. Afterwards he went to a bush and dug out a root and gave it to me.

'This is *fo/ōä,*' he said. 'It's a man's hunting plant, which is also why this is called Hunter's Cave, because it grows only here. When you hunt, you rub a bit on your arms. It makes the animal forget to be afraid.'

He handed it to me and we walked back over the mountains to the hut. I was cross that whole way. I thought he was just making a fool of me and not telling me anything useful, just stuff about clicks and roots. Back at the hut I went to sleep, exhausted. Next morning I asked Zimry: 'Is that the whole story?'

He laughed. 'That is only the beginning of the beginning.'

'So could you tell me more?' He nodded. Then I thought: 'Oh no! We'll have to walk right back to Hunter's Cave.' But instead he led the way into the cave behind the hut. There he started again.

In Red World the people became hungry. The eland fed them fat from their bodies and they became strong. /Kaggen would not eat the fat and he got thin, but he became even cleverer. He stole the songs of the people. They became unhappy with that and wanted to move up again. First Man put his stones on the four corners and the Water Stone in the centre and they all moved up into White World. There they met the Pawed People, who are cats. They were /knã, *the Lion People. And* !nwerri, *the Leopard People. They didn't welcome the Early Race.*

/Kaggen borrowed Blue Agate from First Man and went hunting a rain bull. He caught it with a silver thread. He cut the belly of the animal over the Pawed People. It rained and rained and they became afraid and stopped disturbing the Early

Race, who then forgave /Kaggen for stealing their songs.

There they also found Salt Man and Salt Woman. Also many frogs and lizards and snakes. The name of the frogs was //kwi. *The snakes were* !gu:kan, *the puffadder, and* !kori, *the black cobra with the hood. /Kaggen stopped the people harming them because they were Rain's things.*

The people lived there for a season. Then they wanted to go up again. First Man took the four clouds in his belt and placed them at the four corners. He placed all his treasure stones in the centre and the people were taken up into Blue World. They came out through a crack in a rock. It was in a cave where two rivers crossed. Outside the cave they found seeds. They ate them and this gave them the power to have sex and multiply their numbers. They also found Antelope People: !kwai, *Partridge People:* kottan, *and other animals like* /nabba, *the Zebra People, and* koro, *the Jackal People. There were also huge bulls called* !kwa *that lived in the clouds. These they could control using the treasure stones and also the breath of First Man. They caught them with long, silver threads.*

In Blue World, First Man and First Woman gave birth to Changing Woman. She grew up in nine days and was more clever than all the people except /Kaggen and Jackal, who became her friends. This world had shelters and caves and hunting grounds. It also had a sky and underground which the Early People could travel to through the waterpits and portals in the cave walls. The people decided to stay in this world but they asked First Man to keep the treasure stones and the rolled-up cloud columns safe in case they wanted to move up again.

Zimry took a piece of root out of a bag hanging off his belt and rubbed it on his arms. Then he began singing '*kwesetan, kwesetan*' softly, over and over. I saw a movement out of the corner of my eye and looked at the cave wall. About ten lizards were creeping towards him, shaking their heads up and down. He put down his hand and one walked onto it. He stopped chanting and the lizards all ran away. Then he said: 'You need to know the names of each animal in their own language and they'll come to you. It's not difficult.'

'What about dassies?' I asked him.

'They're named */hun*, remember?' he said, and walked away.

Next day, I asked him to show me about dassies but he just went 'Hmm' and didn't. He could really make me mad.

Each day it was my job to fetch water down at the stream. Well, it wasn't really my job but I did it once, then Zimry never did it again. I was sitting by the water when I decided to see if I could call some frogs. I tried to remember if Zimry had told me their name but couldn't, so I went back and asked him.

'It's *//kwi*,' he said. 'And don't forget your *fo/ōä*.'

I remembered the root he'd dug out for me and fetched it from next to my sleeping mat where I'd dropped it. Back at the stream, I cut a bit of the root and wiped it on my arms and began to chant: '*//kwi*, *//kwi*, *//kwi*'. It sounded silly and I was glad nobody was listening. I wondered why Pieter Kwi got his name and if it had anything to do with calling frogs. The idea of Pieter being a frog caller was funny. But I kept chanting anyway. Suddenly, a frog jumped right onto me. It was a fat one. I first got a big fright, then I was so excited I ran up the hill, spilling a lot of the water and shouted at Zimry: 'I called a frog! I called a frog!' He just said: 'Ja, frogs come quickly,' and he went on cutting a stick. Like it was just normal that I made a frog jump into my lap.

The nights were getting colder. In the city I hadn't noticed it was autumn. It's not important there. You just put on a coat when it gets cold and maybe a beanie. The rain can sometimes be a nuisance, making big puddles between the blocks of flats.

But in the mountains it was different. I found it hard to get out of the blankets in the morning and during the night the cold came up through the sleeping mat. Every few days we cut grass and pushed it under the mats. This made the mat more comfortable and I was cross that Zimry hadn't showed me that when I arrived.

'Why didn't you tell me about the grass before?' I asked him.

'Some things are obvious,' he replied, 'and, anyway, winter's only beginning.'

But still the cold came up. The big problem was that I had no clothes for bad weather. I'd come over the mountains with what I'd run away in and the old coat Mr Kabbo had lent me. My only pair of socks had holes and I wore them until they were just a nuisance and then threw them in the fire. My Nikes were wearing down and one cracked. I had to wind string round the front to keep it from flapping.

I often sat outside the cave in the sun. Sitting there I thought a lot about my Ma. She's so poor and all her life she's been a domestic, working in rich people's houses, cleaning and cooking for them and looking after their children. When I was small she had to get our neighbour to look after me while she went to care for white people's kids. Because transport is bad she had to wake up in the dark to go to the station. But before she left she'd take time to make food for me. Often she only came home when the streetlights were on, so tired. There were bad times when people she worked for left town and she would have days in the week without work. Then the money was little. There was also a family that accused her of stealing and fired her. My Ma, stealing! She would never do a thing like that. Even now she has Thursdays without work. She would get cross with me for running round in the streets and I'd yell at her that she was never home. Then she would cry and I'd feel bad. But I didn't often say sorry or try to make her feel better. I don't know why. I sat in the cave feeling like a dog for that. She was the only person in the world that loved me and I was missing her badly.

If I ever asked her about my Pa, she would just say: 'That's old history. He was a nice man but he went away.' She never even told me his name. She said she was young then and couldn't remember him. After a while I stopped asking her. She once said I was the best thing that ever happened to her. When I remembered that I cried, because I'd given her so much worry and trouble going with the gangs. But you can't *not* be in a gang. I couldn't live in our part of Bonteheuwel without joining or I'd get beaten up or killed. And to get to school I needed to go through the Fancy Boys' territory so I had to go with them sometimes or I'd never reach school. Where Cliffie lived, it was Scorpions territory and we both hung out with them sometimes.

I joined the Blood Brothers in high school because they're the strongest gang in Bonteheuwel. I was small so they got me to go through the windows of empty houses and then open the front door so they could steal stuff. It was really scary and sometimes there was an alarm and we had to run. Sometimes we'd break car windows with a spark plug and get the CD players. If you're not friendly with the gangs, it can be terrible. They're your protection. Now I was sitting in the mountains because Akker wanted to kill me. Some protection! It wasn't a life. I felt weak and really sorry for myself. That's when I got sick. First it was a bad headache. Zimry boiled some leaves and twigs.

'It's called *kooigoed*,' he said. 'It doesn't taste too good.' He was right about that, but it fixed me for a while. Next my chest was sore and the headache came back and I was so weak I couldn't get off the sleeping mat. I felt terrible and the pain in my chest made it hard to breathe.

Zimry took his herb bag and went out for what felt like

days. Maybe it was only hours. I was really going funny in my head. The hut seemed to get very far away, with me huge. Then it would be big and close right on top of me. There were voices and I heard them saying my name. The frogs at the stream were making so much noise if I could stand up I would have thrown stones at them. Birds were screaming and made my ears hurt. I wanted my Ma. There was no hospital and no doctor. I couldn't walk over the mountains. I couldn't even walk out the door!

Zimry came back with rolled-up grass that didn't look like pills. He banged it with a stone and the noise nearly made my head burst. Then he boiled it and threw in some other stuff – he seemed to be doing it so far away but he was in the room. It also tasted bad. I felt I was going to be sick but he must have known and said: 'Don't throw up!' So I didn't. Afterwards I slept, but it wasn't like sleep.

I'm in the cave above the hut and it's full of people with no clothes on. They're beautiful but are also strange, because each one seems to be at the front end of a row of glowing people shapes that are plaited together. The shapes go right out the cave and down the hill. When I look hard there are people shapes all over the valley too. They're very restless and want me to go outside with them, and I do.

They make me lie down under a bush with red flowers. I know it's called kankerbos. *It has long, white stems with lots of leaves coming off them like chutes. The people shapes say this is a test and I have to make a drop of dew come up over the stem and into my mouth without letting it roll off the leaf. They say if I can manage, I'll be able to walk through rock into the Other Side. I can't think how to do that. How do you make a drop of dew roll uphill? But I want to pass the test so I lie there, with them all watching, and try to make the drop move just by concentrating on it. After a bit it wobbles, then starts to move up the stem, but that gets me so excited I stop concentrating and it rolls away off the leaf. I move under another stem and try again. After four tries I make the drop fall into my mouth. It tastes like honey and the people all smile. They say: 'Now you can come to us.'*

I thought they meant I was going to die because maybe they were all dead and it gave me such a spook that I woke up. I was sweating and Zimry was sitting next to me with cold water in a pot and a cloth. He wiped me all over, then gave me more of his medicine. I was too scared to go to sleep again, but it was awful being awake because everything was moving close then far. I was very hot.

I must have fallen asleep again as I had another dream.

I'm hunting for honey in a cave. There are bees everywhere but I'm not afraid of being stung. I take the honey in a bag to a place by the river where there are high reeds. I call and a young eland comes out of the reeds. I put the honey in a hollow stone and it eats. Then I go home. But the people there are cross because I have no honey. The next day I go again to fetch honey for the eland but a young boy follows me. When I take the honey he asks if he can look in my bag but I say he can't because I don't want him to see the honey. Then he goes away and I give the honey to my eland.

Later, when I go to find the eland, it isn't in the reeds. I call and look everywhere. Then I see some people over on the hill and they've killed the animal. The young boy is with them. I become very angry because it's my special animal. I shoot arrows at them but their power is too strong and the arrows fly back at me. Then I try to hit them with my stick but they take it and beat me with it. I manage to take a little piece of the eland's liver as I run and use it to make darkness that hides me. I stay in the darkness for a long time, but then I need to see. So I take one of my shoes and throw it up and it becomes the moon and I can see my way home. Then I wake up.

All week I lay there, drinking Zimry's medicine and some soup he made. The people came back and stood around even when I wasn't asleep. Sometimes they put drops of sweet water into my mouth. I talked to them and they said things to me that seemed to make sense then. But, afterwards, I couldn't remember.

'Who are you talking to?' Zimry asked.

'The hut and outside are full of people,' I told him.

He just smiled and said: 'They're your people.'

I got better, of course. I don't know if it was Zimry's medicine or the drops of water or the soup. But, wow, I was *pap* afterwards.

'It was pneumonia,' he told me. Then he said something that made me angry. 'It's very good you got sick. It's part of the Way.' I thought he was telling me I needed to be punished.

'You talk such rubbish,' I shouted. I was feeling too flat to say anything more and I just kept a fierce face. I wanted to go home. He just asked: 'Did you have any dreams?' I didn't want to tell him anything. I felt too weak to talk. He got up and went over to the box he kept his herbs in and took out a bottle that looked like it was full of honey and gave me some in a spoon, like you feed a baby. It was delicious!

'It's *bossiestroop*. I make it from the spring nectar of protea flowers and also from their roots,' he said. It is hard to stay cross with someone who gives you something that tastes nice. 'I'll give you that twice a day and you'll soon be strong. Then we can start with lessons.'

That sounded really bad to me. Was he going to start teaching me maths and Afrikaans and science and things?

'Now, tell me what you dreamed.'

I told him about the eland and the honey and the shoe

that made the moon. When I'd finished he just thought for a bit, drawing patterns in the sand with a stick, then said: 'This is a big dream. It's the sort you must always tell me. Do you remember what I told you about /Kaggen, the Keeper of All Directions? You're dreaming /Kaggen dreams. Do you understand?'

'No. I don't.

'The eland was /Kaggen's favourite creation,' he said. 'He loved it above all other animals because it knew the way to the time of the Early Race. Your dream is also a story that's been handed down to us from the Early Times, the times of the !Khwe, and it's interesting you're dreaming it now. We have all been many people but we've forgotten. Some people can remember back a few lives, but your dream is coming from a long way back. It's a dream of the beginning of things. You must understand that even when you're walking on that far mountain over there you are never alone. The *n!ao* of all the creatures and the trees and grass and rocks is stroking you. All the people of your family, going back into the beginning of time, are with you. If you know how, you can dream their dreams and they can tell you where you come from. They're your real family.'

When he finished talking, I was crying and, it was odd, I didn't really know why, I think it was the idea of having a big family. I felt safe somehow. This feeling just came up inside me and poured out as tears. Maybe it was just because Zimry was *talking* to me. And I can remember exactly what he said as though he's speaking. Even now. I asked him what I should do about the dream and he said dreams are not about doing, they're about *being*. I should do what I felt was right to do.

For quite a few days I didn't do much of anything. Zimry kept giving me herbs and *bossiestroop*. One afternoon we were outside in the afternoon sun. It felt good to be warm and not sick. I asked him about the herbs and he said he would show me how to find them. Then we talked a bit about being sick and Zimry asked me about the people I had seen all round. It was strange, I'd forgotten about them. Then I remembered the thing about the dewdrop and the *kankerbos* and I told Zimry about it. I didn't expect what happened next. He got mad at me!

You're as thick as a *taaibos* and you're just wasting time,' he shouted. 'You just don't understand, do you?'

'Understand what? No, I don't understand,' I said. I'd never seen him angry and it was horrible.

'Kabbo sends you here to learn the Old Ways. You get the Sickness of Calling. The ancestors initiate you and you *pass* the initiation! And you act like you're just here to eat my food and drink my *bossiestroop*. You don't even *tell* me about the *kankerbos*.'

'I don't know what's special about the *kankerbos*,' I yelled back. 'I don't know anything about the Old Ways. I don't know what initiation you're talking about. I'm here because I'm hiding away from Akker who wants to blow my brains out. That's what I'm doing here. Which is nothing.'

He looked confused for a moment, then said: 'I don't know anything about Akker or why he should blow your brains out. Kabbo sent you here because he thought you were an initiation candidate.'

I shook my head. Pieter Kwi hadn't even told him about Akker or why I was there. All this time he thought I was some sort of student. It was crazy. No wonder he kept asking strange questions.

'Ky, I want you to understand something,' Zimry said, softly. 'The dream you had in Cape Town was part of one of the Great Dreams of our people. Kabbo recognised it, of course. He sent you here to find out if you had the Gift of Seeing. Maybe you were in some trouble back there but that's not important. You had the Sickness of Calling because that's the beginning of the teaching. The Old Ones, your ancestors, were there to greet you and that's not uncommon. But it is very unusual – I have never heard of it – that they should ask you to pass the Initiation of Dew at the beginning of your training. Unheard of. And you succeeded. Maybe Kabbo didn't make it clear to you, but you are now on a path and if you refuse to walk it, you will become very ill. You'll probably die.'

It was hard to imagine that being shot by Akker was unimportant, but his words sent a shiver down my back. My head wanted to argue with him but my body knew he was telling the truth. I got up and walked to the cave. I was in a bad muddle, I can tell you. Going back was death by nine-mill. Doing nothing, if Zimry was right, was death by illness. And going forward meant some kind of mumbo-jumbo thing with this strange man. Every way was frightening. I didn't want to think about it.

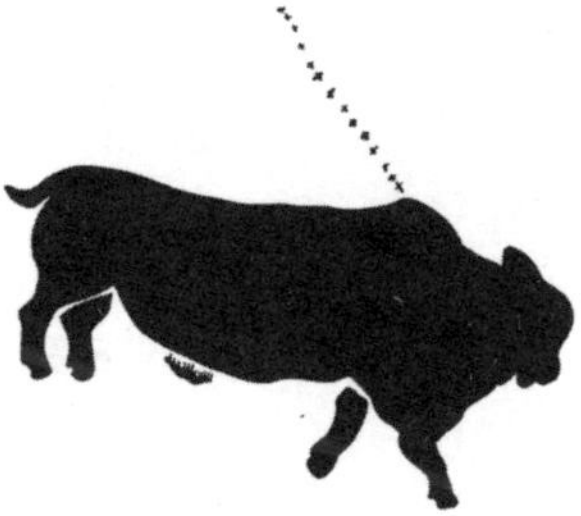

Two days later, Pieter Kwi came down into the valley with bags on his back. A whole month had gone by, but I'd lost track of time. It was strange to see another person. I felt uncomfortable and sort of shy. I wanted to know what was happening and whether I could go home. Pieter wasn't in a hurry to tell me. He asked Zimry about his health and mine also. Zimry told him I'd been ill. Pieter pointed to one bag saying 'It's for you. Your mother packed it.' I jumped and unzipped it. It was clothes and my coat and boots and also soap and toothpaste and a razor and all sorts of useful things like my pocket knife and a plate and forks. There was also a note. It said: 'Dearest Ky, I hope you are well. I miss you. Please don't come home yet. It is not safe. Here are some things for you. I love you. Ma.'

Pieter was watching me read. 'Did your Ma say you should stay here?' he asked.

'Ja, she said I mustn't come home.'

She's right,' he nodded and said: 'It's hard for her. There's a big hunt going on. The Tough Livings are out for revenge. They've declared war on the Blood Brothers and you're the man they're after.'

I realised while he was talking that I'd never believed I

would be staying for more than a month. Just then I felt like a man who'd heard a judge tell him he was going to prison for life. I walked away. Inside I had a boiling feeling. It was like my head would explode. I couldn't do anything. I just felt sad and kind of dizzy. When Pieter left I was still on my own. Zimry came behind me and put his hand on my shoulder.

'There's a black eagle. It's the same one you saw when Pieter brought you,' he said. 'You see it over there? Up above the cedars. It's a good sign. Pieter brought us some food. Let's go see what's good to eat.' We went back towards the hut and, it was strange, I suddenly felt a great peace inside me. It didn't make sense.

The food was delicious. There were two Tupperwares with *frikkadels* and *sosaties* and a *babotie* my Ma had cooked. There were also apples – I never realised until then how good apples taste. And small packs of rice and flour and sugar and potatoes. Pieter must be a strong man to carry all that over the mountain. Right at the bottom of the sack were two bars of chocolate. Later, me and Zimry watched the sun go down and ate a whole slab. It was like heaven. Chocolaty sweet, and the sunbirds talking in the proteas and the sun all soft and yellow so you could look straight at it.

'Why does Kabbo know about dreams?' I asked Zimry. 'Why did he send me to you?'

He didn't answer right away. I had learned that if he took a long time I'd asked a big question. He fetched his pipe and some dry weed and sat there flicking the seeds into a hollow in the rock. Then he lit it and puffed away, staring at the valley.

'Kabbo is a Keeper of the Old Ways,' he said at last. 'There aren't enough like him. The First People, the Old Ones, they knew many things about the earth and the plants and animals. They knew how the stars worked and also the moon. They were the children of Changing Woman and of /Kaggen. Africa had been their home all that time until just a little while ago when black people and then white people came.'

Zimry began sorting his weed again, picking out seeds and pushing the stuff into his old pipe. It seemed like he'd finished his story and I couldn't work out what it had to do with Kabbo or me.

'What's Kabbo care about all this?' I asked.

'For thousands of years there have been people who've been going to the place we call the Other Side, the other side of death. They're the Keepers. Each had certain work to do, areas to look after. They couldn't control the earth, it's much too powerful. But they nudged things. They nudged clouds to make rain. They gave some power to species who were struggling. Like gardening.

'The One God people – the white missionaries who didn't know the Spirit was in everything – were afraid of the power of the Keepers. They hated them. They took over their lands. The soldiers who came with them killed Keepers. The missionaries called Keepers witches and demons and evil people. In only a few hundred years, colonial troops killed thousands of our people and also the Keepers with them. And the earth is hurt because it has so few gardeners and keepers of the *n!ao*.

'When the Old Ones saw what was happening, they said: 'We must save the Old Ways until we are free again. Because if we don't, the white and black man will destroy them.' For thousands of years my people had painted on rock walls. But they weren't just pictures. They were instructions. These the /Xam couldn't hide. But they saw the missionaries didn't understand what they meant. So they told those who could travel through the rock to heal or make rain to hide their knowledge. They should only do it in secret so we wouldn't lose the path of the Old Ones, the doors to the Other Side.

'Black and white people know many things,' he went on. 'They make guns and cars and aeroplanes. They make war also. But they don't know how to speak to the earth. They don't know how to listen to the language of trees. Or the birds or the eland. If you can't talk to life, you can't hear it either. Without that talk, the earth will kill us all in the end because we'll injure it and make life impossible. Whites and blacks can't hear the voices in the stars like we can.

'The earth isn't good for us just by chance. Plants take the bad air and make it so we can breathe. Life makes the sky so the sun doesn't burn us up. Elephants ate the forests so there'd be grasslands for the buck and places where we could hunt them. The First People, who weren't as we are today, learned to be humans on the grasslands. It's all connected. Not just chance.' Zimry was rambling all over the place, but he wasn't answering my question.

'What about me?' I asked.

'Today we teach those who we recognise. And often we recognise them by dreams or sickness. We're the Keepers. Kabbo's a Keeper. I'm the Keeper of the Southern Sand World, which they call fynbos. It's the area up the West Coast to Angola and also the Kalahari.'

'So Kabbo thought my dream was a sign?' I asked. 'Even if I think it was just a dream.'

'He recognised you as San,' Zimry said.

'What do you mean?

'You're /Xam. A Bushman.'

I tell you, that was too much. I'd nearly killed Akker for insulting me like that. I felt a rage that was big and frightening.

'No!' I shouted and jumped up. I saw points of light flickering in my eyes. Then the most amazing thing happened. The valley filled up with people again. The same ones with the shimmery trails. They were all walking round in the twilight and even up to us. I got such a shock I ran into the hut and ate half the second bar of chocolate we'd agreed to save. I don't know why. I was shaking with anger but also really scared of all those things outside. I lay on my bed and just sulked. Zimry came in and asked what was going on. I told him about the people. He smiled.

'Look at them closely. They're your ancestors. And your ancestors' ancestors. They're always with you. When you swallowed the drop of dew, you opened the door to their world. It was the drop of the Water Stone. They'll never hurt you. You're their body in this world.'

I was scared to go to sleep that night. I didn't want my ancestors to go walking round in my dreams. I heard owls, and then a jackal. It made me shiver all over. But I did sleep. Next morning, when I opened my eyes, the sun was shining and all that stuff seemed far away. Even silly. The sun makes you brave.

'You never really told me how to catch a dassie,' I said when Zimry came back from the river. 'You said you would and you didn't. All I got was a frog.'

'You do it the same way as the frog,' said Zimry. 'But dassies are smarter than frogs. They have strong minds. You have to go into their world to catch them. Call them by name.'

'So how do I go into their world?' I asked. 'Isn't it this world?'

Zimry shook his head. 'Everything lives in its own world. Even you aren't in the same world as me. But you can enter their world with your spirit. Let me show you something. Sit right in front of me and look at me. Don't think of anything.'

I sat looking at him but it was impossible not to think of anything. I was looking at his *peperkorreltjies* and his little beard and thinking he was really funny-looking. It's not easy looking into a person's eyes like that. He had wrinkles all round them and then I noticed they were really kind. And his brown part, his eye colour, was so deep it seemed I could look right into his head. Then something strange happened. My mind sort of went *whoosh* and he became young. He still had *peperkorreltjies* and the same light, almost yellow skin, but his eyes were young and not wrinkly. Then I realised I wasn't looking at him but at me. I opened my mouth and the 'me' also opened his, like looking into a mirror. I got such a *skrik*. I jumped up and then fell over a pot and landed on my backside. Zimry was laughing like he could split his sides.

'What happened?' I yelled. 'What did you do to me?'

He laughed some more and I thought he would just talk about something else like he does when I ask him things. But he made me sit down and he looked serious.

'Our minds are outside our heads. Maybe our brains are inside, but our minds are outside. All of this is your mind,' he said, waving his hand in a circle. 'And also mine. We're connected that way. Our minds can circle each other. Then you can look back at yourself because you're in the other mind. It's not difficult to understand.

'I'm looking old these days. All those wrinkles,' he said. I realised Zimry didn't have a mirror in his hut. It was funny to think of him using me as a mirror, I started to giggle. We just sat there laughing at each other. Then I remembered the dassies.

'So how do you catch a dassie?'

'Dassies don't have minds like ours but they're very curious. Call them by their name and circle them with your mind like we just did. They'll come to you. Remember, their name is */hun* and they're from the Red World. But also use your *fo/ōä* root. That makes them forget you're a danger to them. And be still. You're a hunter.'

That was exciting! I cut off a small piece of *fo/ōä*, rubbed some on my arms and went up the hill to the cliff where there were dassies. I perched on the rock. As still as a lizard. When a dassie was nearby, I began chanting its name quietly. He was watching me. I called him for a bit and he scrambled right up to me. I grabbed him behind the neck and ran down to Zimry, the dassie kicking and squeaking in my hands. I didn't know what to do with it. Zimry was really pleased. He was grinning like mad. I handed him the dassie but he shook his head.

'I think let it go. It is a small one and there's not much meat on it. But when you catch a big one, it is you who must kill it, because it's given its life to you and not to me. You just break its neck, click, quickly.'

It sounded horrible. I was used to buying food at the shop and Zimry had done all the catching up to now. I let the dassie go and it ran away fast. The rest of the day I felt good. I was a dassie hunter.

The first time I killed a dassie, it was terrible. It was a big one and Zimry hadn't caught anything so we needed it. I twisted its head and pulled and I could feel its spine crack. It stopped kicking and then it was just meat, hanging in my hand, all warm and furry. After that Zimry didn't catch dassies. If I didn't call them we didn't eat, so I became the hunter. The bad part was that I had to gut and skin them as well. Zimry showed me which parts to cut and what to put out for the hawks and crows. I became quite good at it, but it was always yuck.

The real problem wasn't dassie, though, but all the creepy crawlies around the place. We used to get cockroaches in Bonteheuwel, and, in summer, mosquitoes. But in the mountains there were big spiders and hairy centipedes that could bite and long, brown songololos. Even the ants were dangerous. One day I sat on a patch of ground without grass and something bit my leg. I jumped up and suddenly burning bites were happening all over my legs and in my pants. There were little red fire ants all over me. I beat at them and jumped around but they were still biting. So I took off all my clothes and ran down to the river and jumped in. When I looked back at the hut, Zimry was rolling on the ground laughing. I didn't think it was funny. The red bites lasted for days.

One day I found a big, skinny green thing sitting on a rock in front of the hut. I pulled of a shoe to give it a whack but Zimry caught my arm.

'Don't *ever* kill those,' he said. 'Never ever.'

'What is it?' I asked.

'A praying mantis. It's /Kaggen's messenger. Remember the story I told you? Mantis is another name for /Kaggen. Maybe it's what he becomes to travel in the world.'

'It looks mean,' I said.

'Mantis is many things,' he said, picking it up gently, 'but he's not mean.' He held it out towards me. It turned its head to look at me with its big eyes and waved its long feelers like it was sending signals. I didn't know insects could do that. It felt a bit spooky to be looked at so closely by such a little thing.

One day Zimry said he had to go away for a while. That really freaked me. How could I stay in this wild place all alone? Why did he have to go?

'I'm a game warden,' he said. 'I have to meet rangers and talk about conservation. We are in a wilderness area. It's a sort of park.'

I'd become used to the badges on his shoulders and his khaki clothes, but I thought it was just that he liked wearing them. I hadn't realised he was working. I asked him all sorts of questions. What was his job? What did he do?

'I make inventories,' he said. 'When I go out walking I check plants and animals, the state of the rivers. I listen for types of frogs. I check what's there and what's missing and how things are doing in the seasons. And things aren't right. They're changing fast. Summer and winter aren't the same as they used to be. The rain is often in the wrong place or doesn't come at all. The sun's getting too hot. Things are starting to disconnect. Some plants are dying lower down and growing on hills instead of where they used to grow.

'Rainfall is changing. Tortoises are moving away. The wrong ants are down in the valley here, little black ones that don't plant seeds like the other ants do. The song of the moss frog has disappeared. I haven't seen the bees that pollinate the green-ivory orchid for two seasons. There's something going wrong with the Sand World and it's affecting these mountains. But I don't know exactly what. Weather patterns are forgetting to *be* patterns. The threads are coming loose. I have to report all these things and talk about them with the other rangers.'

'I haven't seen you writing this down.'

'I can't write. I remember everything.'

'You can't *write*? What do you mean?'

'I never went to school. I wasn't taught to write. I learned to remember instead.'

'Even the number of plants and dassies? All the bulbs and frogs and things here you *count*?'

'Yes. I mark areas with pegs and tape and count how many of each plant there is inside them. The smaller animals are more difficult. But I just watch certain cliffs or check tracks in the sand. I also count birds, mainly raptors. I search for geometric and tent tortoises.'

I'd seen the tape squares but I thought they were part of Zimry's magic. I suppose they were. Then I thought about being alone and I started to panic. I'm not sure what I imagined would happen, just being the only person in this huge place, maybe. I asked if I could come with him but he refused.

'The park doesn't know you're here,' he said. 'It's best they don't know. I'll only be a few days.'

Zimry packed his rucksack, waved and was gone before the sun was up the next day. It tore a hole in my world. Zimry doesn't make much noise, but without him it was too quiet. Every time a duiker snorted or an eagle screamed, I'd jump, my heart thumping. I didn't know what to do. I mean, there wasn't much entertainment out there. Zimry was my TV. That night I awoke with light streaming through the window. I lay there in sleepiness puzzling whether it was morning, then got up, pulled a blanket around me and went outside. It wasn't dawn but a full moon, so bright I could see the mountains clearly and the cliffs behind the hut. I stared at the moon and saw patterns on it like a rabbit. An owl went *hooo* and far away a nightjar made its funny skipping call. Then I thought about leopards and went back inside.

The first day Zimry was away was long. I watched the sun come up and flood into the valley, making the river shine like a silver ribbon. In town you get people and buildings and noise going on all the time. In the mountains there was probably nobody for further than I could see. The only building was Zimry's hut.

Being alone like that seemed to turn me inside out. I wasn't thinking *me* thoughts, just watching and listening. When a grasshopper jumped with a *zzzt*, I watched it all the way to where it landed. Far away a baboon went *bahooo* and others shouted back at him. It seemed to become a fight, with screeches and barking that went on for quite a while. Up on the cliffs two starlings must have been defending their nest. Every time a crow or hawk flew over, they'd go for it and try to peck it from behind. They did that for hours. They never seemed to get tired. I spent a long time watching a cloud change shape. First it looked like a fat animal with a big mouth, then it began stretching into a bird. Its tail got longer and it became a lizard.

That made me remember I could call lizards and got one to jump onto my hand. Afterwards I dipped in the river, even though it was freezing. Later I realised I hadn't eaten anything and I went up near the cave to see if I could find a dassie. There were none around so I hoped maybe one would turn up. I was there for ages. After a while I thought about Auri and wondered if I'd ever see her again. For some reason her name made me remember *!nwerri*, the name Zimry told me leopards were called. I was playing with the word in my mind when a small sound, like *rrrr*, made me look sideways at the edge of the cave and I tell you my heart nearly stopped. A leopard was standing there.

It was huge, with golden eyes and so close I could see her whiskers moving forward. Somehow I knew it was a she. First I wanted to run away, but I just didn't. She was beautiful and, after getting the first fright, I stopped being scared. She sat down, just like a cat does, and we looked at each other for quite a long time. Suddenly she blinked, got up and walked round the cliff and was gone. After that my mind went blank. Then I got excited because I thought maybe I had called her.

I didn't get to eat anything that day, just a bit of old fire bread. I'm not sure why, because there were things I could eat if I wanted to. I went to sleep and had a dream.

I'm running away from a lion through the valleys of the Chameleon Mountains. My shoulder hurts where a lion bit me, but I have to get back to my people fast. I know the lion will follow me because he has licked my tears. I run back to the huts and the people gather round me, asking what's happened. When I tell them the story they become terribly afraid, because they say if a lion has licked your tears you are his. He will not be far behind.

I beg my mother to hide me. She gets karosses made from dassie skins, lots of them, and rolls me up in them. Then she puts me in a hut. Soon the lion comes and he asks: 'Where is the hunter?' The people say there's no hunter here. But he says he knows they're lying. He has licked tears and they know it's his right to eat me. They say 'No, no' but he says he will eat them all if they don't give me to him. My mother is crying. But she knows the lion will do that, so she fetches me in the karosses and rolls me out towards the lion. I get dizzy from the rolling, and when I look up, there is the lion. As he pounces on me I wake up.

The dream made me nervous and I thought about the leopard and how thin the door of the hut was. When I went half to sleep afterwards, the hut filled with the people with the shimmery trails. It was a bad night.

Zimry was away for three days. When he came back there was a man with him. I thought it was someone come to arrest me because he was also in khaki, and when I saw them coming I ran into the cave. But you can't hide anything from Zimry. He shouted: 'Hey, Ky! Come down. I want you to meet Steve.'

The man put out his hand and shook mine. His was big, like the paw of the lion I dreamed about. Zimry said Steve knew about rock art and had come to look for caves. He had a tent and a pack full of food and all sorts of things, like sketchbooks and a bag of pens and brushes. Also a camera.

I wanted to tell Zimry about the leopard right away but I couldn't because the man was there. I waited until we'd had something to eat and Steve had put up his tent and gone to sleep. Then I said to Zimry: 'I called a leopard.'

'How?' He was startled.

'I said its name and a leopard came.'

'I haven't taught you to do that yet,' he snapped, under his breath so Steve wouldn't hear. Then he really *skelled* me out. I thought he'd be proud of me.

'You could have been hurt, maybe even killed,' he said. 'What would I do then?' He looked at me, his eyes all fierce. Then he did something amazing. He stepped round the fire and hugged me. I want to tell you it blew me away. The only men I knew were the gang leaders round the flats and maybe some schoolteachers who weren't really worth much. Mostly I spent time with my street brothers. I didn't really talk to any men. When Zimry hugged me I realised I didn't even know what a man was, if you get what I mean. I didn't know they were the kind of people who hugged anyone. I just stood there, shocked, and then tears ran down my face. Like a baby. I suddenly felt so empty about not having a father, but all my life I never knew that I wanted one.

Zimry gave me a sort of gentle thump on my chest with his fist and said: 'It's okay. It's okay. Just don't call your leopard too often. We might lose our supply of dassies. Now, tell me, did you have any dreams while I was away?' I told him about the lion and the kaross. He didn't say anything for a long time after that. I thought he'd forgotten about me. Then he said: 'You know that was another part of the dream Kabbo sent you here with?'

'Yes.'

'It is also part of one of the Great Dreams of our people,' he said. 'You have only seen part of it but you've been there twice and the story's connected. It's a dream of Making. I can't tell you more because it needs to come from inside you. Kabbo was right to send you. Tonight you've made an old man happy.' He got up and began to walk to the hut. Suddenly, he turned to me and said: 'Maybe you're the one of whom they speak.'

'Who speaks?' I said. But Zimry wasn't listening to questions.

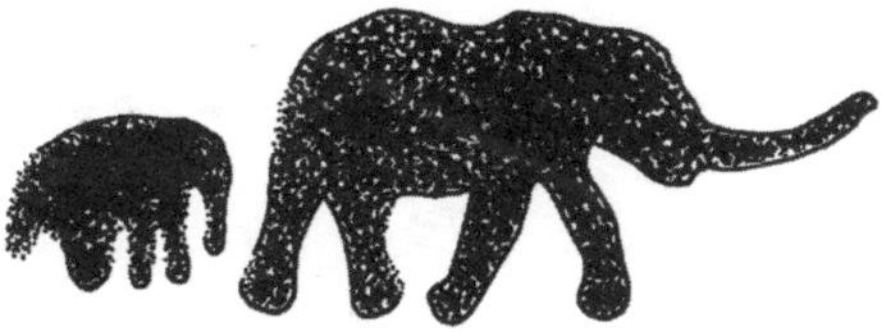

Next morning Steve asked me if I'd help him find shelters with paintings in them. He was a really friendly guy and it was nice to have someone else and not just Zimry. I agreed. Also, after Hunter's Cave, I had a strange excitement about seeing more rock art. We walked over the hill in front of the hut, then over another and into a valley full of strange rocks. They seemed like a whole ruined city – blocks but all rough like they'd been in the sun too long. It wasn't that far away but I'd never been there before. All the time we walked Steve talked about the /Xam people and how amazing their art was and how sad that they weren't around any more.

He was so busy with all this stuff that he didn't ask anything about me, which was good because I wasn't about to tell him my life history or anything. Also, I still wasn't sure that if he found out why I was there, he wouldn't cause trouble or tell someone. He had a backpack and binoculars that he kept looking through. I wasn't saying much.

Steve told me he was an artist and that he'd fallen in love with rock art and wanted to find all the places it was painted in these mountains. It sounded strange that a whitey was running all over the place looking for rock paintings. I asked him if he'd seen Hunter's Cave.

'You've seen that cave?' he asked. I thought maybe I wasn't supposed to have been there.

'Zimry took you?'

'Yes,' I nodded, hoping I wasn't getting Zimry into trouble.

Steve laughed and said: 'You must be very special. It's a sacred site. There can't be many people who have been there.' I felt good that Zimry had taken me, even though it had made me cross at the time.

We walked into the mess of rocks and it was *spooky* in there. Really strange. There were piles with more piles on top of them, like pillars, and rough. It was so quiet that when an insect buzzed I jumped. We walked round some rocks and up high was a whole row of caves. The way the sun was shining on the rock, with shadows between the columns, made it look like a picture I once saw of a church's organ's pipes. There were holes in the rock that seemed like eyes, looking down at us. If Steve hadn't been there I would have run like hell. But he just went, 'Wow!' and kept climbing up towards the cliff. He walked into the biggest cave with me far enough behind that if a leopard sprang out of the cave I could jump onto one of the rocks, but not too far because it felt as if something was following us.

When I went into the cave it was dark after the bright sunlight and smelled like dassie piss. Steve was kneeling at the back, staring at the rock and going: 'Yeah, yeah, yeah.' There were blobs of colour on the rock he said were eland, but they didn't look like anything at all to me.

'They're red because red ochre sticks to the rock best,' he said. 'The white clay fades and lichen turns colours all black. These paintings are maybe thousands of years old. Look at these people with antelope heads. They're in trance. And there, this has faded but you can see it's an elephant.'

'What do you mean trance?' I asked.

'The shamans would dance, round and round a fire, until they left their bodies. They said trance felt like they were stretching. They also often took on the bodies of animals to go through into the spirit world. The favourite was the eland. So they painted long, thin people with eland heads. Here. Look,' he pointed. 'These have antelope heads. And the dots and lines are connections and energies. It's a brilliant way of showing what it feels like in trance.'

It was strange, because the more he talked, the more pictures I could make out on the rock. 'What do you think these paintings are about?' he asked.

'It looks like there are people hunting the eland and the painter made a mistake by drawing them on top of an elephant.'

'Probably not,' Steve said. 'This is a rainmaking picture. They're shamans going into the spirit world. The elephant's a rain cloud they're pulling to bring rain where there's drought. They're people who ride the rain.'

It sounded silly to me. He was going on just like Zimry. 'How could anyone pull a cloud, especially skinny little people with buck heads?' I thought. 'And why would an elephant be a cloud?' We went into another cave and there was a painting of sausage shapes next to each other and all around them hundreds of little dots.

'These are termite mounds,' he said. 'Termite eggs were special food for the /Xam. They were called Bushman rice. But also the mounds were sacred places because that's where /Kaggen sometimes hid.'

I said: 'Ja, I know all about Bushman rice. I ate some.'

There were a few other caves but they had no paintings. Some were quite hard to get into and I noticed that everywhere I put my hand to pull myself up or stop myself falling it was very shiny, even though the rest of the rock was rough.

'Why's this so shiny?' I asked.

'After thousands of years of people doing just what you're doing, of course the rock gets shiny. You may be putting your hands in the places of your ancestors.'

We left the caves and walked down a gap between the high rocks. Steve was looking all over with his binoculars, then he pushed behind a bush and there was a rock overhang with more paintings. They seemed to be of a group of women because you could see their tits and they had their hands up clapping. Some men with their pricks standing up were dancing, but all bent over. 'It's a trance dance,' said Steve.

I was tired from walking and also pissed off with Steve saying these Bushmen were my ancestors, just like he knew everything. I was tired of Zimry's /Xam stuff and I was missing home. I just said: 'That's all rubbish. How do you know what they're doing? They're just dancing.'

'See the blood coming out of their noses,' he said. 'When Bushmen go into trance they bleed like that. And also they bend over because they get cramps in their stomachs. It's the Dance of Blood. Hasn't Zimry told you about that?'

Ja, well, that did it. I don't know why. I shouted at him: 'You don't even know any Bushmen. They went away hundreds of years ago. They've gone. Disappeared. There aren't any. Why do you and Zimry and everyone keep going on about Bushmen? They're just *Hotnots*.'

Steve looked hurt. He said: 'I'm sorry. I thought you were Zimry's apprentice. He said to tell you about these things.'

I was all upside-down inside. I pushed out of the overhang and just ran between the rocks. I didn't know where I was going. Steve shouted: 'You'll get lost.' But I didn't care. I was fighting this Bushman thing. At school, before I joined the Blood Brothers so they were too afraid to say it to my face, people laughed about my hair and my skin colour and my size. And I was now in the middle of nowhere and people were still doing it. It was too much.

I don't know how I ended up in the cave. I was really tired from running and it was cool and I just sat down. I was crying. About everything. It sounds funny now, but I wanted to see my Ma. When my eyes were working properly again I looked at the rock next to me and got such a shock I banged my head on the low roof. The cave was full of paintings. There were eland and people with buck heads and zigzags and dots and even red handprints like I used to do when I started school. But what really spooked me was that there was a *kankerbos* like the one I saw when I was sick and someone lying under it with his mouth open. I could see it was a man because he had his cock pricked up. And next to that painting was a whole row of people all standing behind each other.

I don't know why I did it, but I reached up and put my hand over a red hand on the rock. What happened next was weird. I felt dizzy and couldn't pull my hand away, like the wall was a magnet. The painted people got bright and went back and back, like there was no rock wall. There were dots and funny little ziggy lines that seemed to be inside my eyes but also on the rock. I think I screamed. It felt like I was stretching and stretching then falling through the rock. That doesn't make sense when I tell you here, but that rock felt like a hole that went on forever. All the time there were silvery people around me.

I don't know what happened after that. When I woke up, Zimry and Steve were there. They had a wet cloth and were wiping me all over. It felt nice to be cool. They looked worried and, maybe just because it was good to be alive, I laughed.

'It's not funny,' Zimry said. 'You're crazy. You'll kill me with being so careless.'

Afterwards, back at the hut, Steve told me he had spent hours calling me. 'I looked in every cave and overhang and even in holes under rocks,' he said. 'When I found you I thought you were dead, because you were lying there with blood coming out your nose. I saw you'd hit your head. I couldn't carry you over all those rough rocks but I checked your pulse and it was okay.'

He'd then run all the way to Zimry and all the way back with him. I couldn't imagine Zimry running. I could see Zimry wanted to be cross but I was so weak his worry side beat his cross side.

That night I slept a black sleep and felt much better in the morning. I was so hungry I ate a lot of Steve's food. 'What happened?' asked Zimry when I'd finished eating.

'I don't know,' I said. 'When I touched the handprint I seemed to get stuck to the wall. All the paintings got brighter. Then it felt as though I was falling into a place that had lights flashing all over the place. Next thing you were there.'

Zimry wiped his hand across his face and frowned at me. 'I told Steve you could help him look for caves so I will honour that. But Ky, promise me you won't touch any paintings.' It was an easy promise to make. After what happened, I wasn't going to put my hand near the things.

For the next two weeks Steve and I wandered all over. It was warm and sometimes we slept outside or under an overhang. I would wake up in the night and stare at the band of stars overhead. They seemed so close. If I watched long enough I'd see one of them fall, making a streak across the black sky.

Sometimes we'd wake and be all wet from mist. It would make the morning dark and strange and very quiet. We'd make a fire and sit around it talking until the sun burnt the mist away. Steve told me the band in the sky was called the Milky Way. He said it got that name because it looked like spilled milk. At its centre was a black hole that ate stars. He said if the number of stars was like grains of sand on a beach, earth would be the size of a bit of dust circling a single grain. The Universe was too big to imagine.

After falling through the handprint, though, I somehow

knew where paintings were in all that jumble of cliffs and rocks. I could just feel them. That made Steve happy. I think we discovered about fifty painting sites that had never been found before. One evening, when we were all round the fire talking about my experience in the cave, I called it the Cave of Hands. Steve said it was a good name.

I was sorry when he left. Although I'd shouted at him, we became good friends.

When Auri and her father walked down the hill to our hut I couldn't believe my eyes. She looked so beautiful out there in that wild place. She was wearing a red shirt without sleeves and cargo pants and Hi-Tec boots, like she'd stepped out one of those magazines, though she was panting from the hike. The only people I'd seen for months and months were three men. I wanted to run and hug her but I was shy. I thought she was maybe mad at me for putting her family to such trouble.

'Hi, Ky,' she said and walked up and hugged *me*. Then she pushed me back with her hands on my shoulders saying: 'Phew, you're smelly and I think you need some clean clothes.'

Mr Kabbo shook my hand formally then sat down to talk to Zimry. 'Why are you here?' I asked Auri. 'What's happening back home? Are the Tough Livings still looking for me? What did the school say when I just disappeared? Have you seen my Ma?'

'Whoa, slow down,' she said. 'Too many questions all at once. I've carried heavy bags over these mountains and first I need to drink and I need a rest.' I got all shy again.

'Sorry, sorry, I'm being really rude,' I said. She laughed. Hey, she looked good when she did that, with those eyes that always seem to be smiling and such perfect teeth. I took her down to the stream where she drank like she hadn't seen water for days.

'You look fit, but wild,' she said. 'I'm here because it's holidays and Pa was coming and I asked if I could come too. It's Christmas break. I wanted to see how you were getting along.' That startled me. Christmas meant it was December and I left in April. I'd been in the mountains for nine months but hadn't been counting. Out there all that mattered was heat and cold, rain and sunshine, not weeks or months.

'Yes, the Tough Livings are still looking for you,' she said, and I got a tight feeling in my stomach. 'They think you ran away to the fishing boats. They've been hassling the fishermen at Kalk Bay. At school they know why you left but they didn't ask too many questions. They don't care. And I went to see your Ma. That's why I carried a big bag as well as my backpack. It's stuff from her. You owe me big time.'

Later, in the hut, I unzipped the bag. It was filled with my clothes and a few new ones as well. There was even more chocolate and useful things in the side pockets. I suddenly felt sad for my Ma, because she's poor and still she bought all these things for me. And also because she was alone. 'If you want to wear that stuff you'd better get cleaned up first,' Auri said. 'Otherwise the clothes will jump right off your back.' I said 'Ja' and grabbed a towel out of the bag. It smelled like my Ma and I held it against my nose all the way down to the river. Auri came with, which was a problem because my underpants had given up long ago and I had to get into the water to wash. I put the towel round me and shook off my clothes and jumped into the water quickly, hoping she would look the other way. But, of course, she just kept looking at me. The water was like ice. Then, calmly, like she did it all the time, Auri took off her shirt and pants and jumped in too. That caused me another problem because then I was worrying about how I would get out without her seeing that I was standing up like those men in the rock art.

Auri splashed me and I threw a clay ball at her and we ended up covered in mud and making a lot of noise. Later, she dried herself with my towel, dressed and walked up to the hut while I pretended to swim. Fresh clothes felt like heaven. Ever since the moment I put them on that day, I've looked after clothes like they were my best friends. People say you don't know what you've got till you haven't got it any more. That's too true.

Mr Kabbo had a tent and I helped him put it up near the hut. That night round the fire, Mr Kabbo asked me about things Zimry told him while we were swimming.

'I had another part of the lion dream,' I told him, and he asked me to describe it, which I did. 'Anything else?' he asked.

'I learned how to catch dassies and I called a leopard. Well, I think I called it. And I got sick. Zimry says it was pneumonia. There were silvery people all over and they made me take a test.'

'Ja, Zimry told me that,' he nodded. I was shy about talking in front of Auri but she seemed interested. When we were getting ready to go to bed, Mr Kabbo said something that felt really good. 'Ky, I'm glad you came through Auri's window that night.'

Next morning, we got up early because Mr Kabbo said he'd like to see the Cave of Hands. Zimry was counting wild rosemary plants in his tape squares so he stayed behind. I showed him and Auri the organ pipe cave and I noticed Mr Kabbo didn't just walk into it like Steve. He picked dry leaves from some buchu bushes and lit them. It made a really nice smell. Then he walked into the cave with the smoke going first. He said it was in case there were bad spirits living there. It was quite hard to find the Cave of Hands because I hadn't been thinking about where it was when I first went into it or when I left. But I walked around and eventually found it. We went inside. He and Auri were very quiet in there, just staring at the paintings. It gave me a funny feeling, like I was in a dream, and I made sure I didn't touch any of the paintings. Especially a hand.

When they left a few days later I felt lost without Auri. I wandered round until Zimry told me to do something useful, like catch supper. But I didn't. Everything seemed to lose colour. The green fynbos, the purple mountains, the gold on the rocks were just flat nothing. Missing her made me miss home and I started worrying about how I would ever be able to return. Akker wasn't going to forget about me. I thought about going to Johannesburg. Then I wondered if I could find work in one of the small towns, but that made me even more down.

Zimry watched me mope around for a few days, then he said: 'I want to tell you a story.' I wasn't in the mood for that but he just started talking. When there's nobody else around and the only person for miles starts talking, you kind of have to listen. So I started drawing spirals in the sand with a stick while Zimry rambled on. Slowly, I became interested.

The /Xam say all animals were once people. They came from the First People. They only later became animals. The Aardvark was a person of the Early People and she wanted a child but couldn't get one. So she collected ants' eggs and put them outside her hole where the springbok walked. She knew springbok loved eating dried ants' eggs. When a springbok mother came past with a young one, Anteater asked:

'What kind of child is this?'

The mother, who was not stupid and knew Anteater wanted a girl child, said:

'It is a boy child.'

Anteater asked many springbok mothers, who all answered the same, but then one really stupid springbok came along.

'What kind of child is this?' Anteater asked.

'It's a girl child,' answered the springbok.

'Would you not like to go there and eat those lovely ants' eggs?' said Anteater. 'And while you eat I will hold your lovely child.'

The springbok went. Then the Anteater took the child and ran down her hole. The springbok called and cried and sat by the hole for a long time but eventually left and went home. The springbok's husband was so angry that he struck her on her foot, cracking it in half, which is why springbok have cloven hooves today.

Anteater looked after the little springbok, whose name was Koukou, as though it was her daughter. When she had grown into a teenager, Rooikat was passing by and saw her. He said to himself: 'She must be my wife.' When Anteater was fetching water, Rooikat came to Koukou and said to her:

'You are not an anteater. You are a springbok and you were stolen from your mother.' Then Rooikat hid until the next day. When it was Koukou's turn to fetch water, Rooikat met her at the waterpit and said:

'Come with me. I'll take you to your people.'

So Koukou ran away with Rooikat. But Partridge saw them running and told Anteater, who began to chase them, but underground by burrowing. Rooikat felt the ground shaking and looked back. There he saw the mound of earth Anteater was making and it was coming very fast. They ran but Anteater was coming faster. So Rooikat made a loop with his bow and put it in the path of Anteater, who was caught tight with the string around her neck. Before Rooikat and the springbok could run away, Anteater made a curse which, in the way of the Old People, was terrible. She said:

'You will become a rooikat that hunts at night with no thumbs to pull a bow.'

And it was so.

But Rooikat said: 'You will become an anteater who walks only at night and eats ants. For it is with ants that you tricked the springbok.'

And it was so. The little springbok got a huge fright, jumping high like springbok do, and ran to her people, bouncing, bouncing all the way. When she got to her people they didn't recognise her. They said:

'She is not a person like us. She has bounced and bounced and has become a springbok. But she is very beautiful.'

I laughed. Zimry's stories were such nonsense. He said to me: 'You must always see the story you're in. Your springbok is beautiful and free. Your antbear is stuck in a hole back in the city and you are the family of the Pawed People. Your leopard knew that. I think I must teach you to dance.'

That guy....

I thought Zimry was just playing with words about dancing. But he wasn't. The next day he told me we were going to a village. I didn't know where it was or why we were going. When I asked him, he said: 'That's where you will learn to dance.' When I asked him if they had a club there or something, he laughed until he coughed and then didn't say anything more.

'Get some clothes in your backpack,' he told me. 'And bring some fire bread and anything else you can find to eat.'

We packed and began walking – all day – and it was wild and rough. We went up over a mountain called Krakadouw, then down a valley that had a rock that looked like a dog sitting up, but it was maybe ten stories high. After that we ended up on a road that took us down into flat land with fields of rooibos. There were maybe fifteen little thatched houses with gardens and everywhere were pear trees.

I was very shy walking into the village. I hadn't seen people for so long and I started worrying about smelling funny and with my clothes not really too clean. Someone in a field saw us and shouted: 'Zimreeeee.' The whole place was yelling and running round with dogs barking. I didn't know how to deal with all the noise after how quiet the mountains had been. But everyone ignored me. They were treating Zimry like he was famous. They took us into a house and made coffee and rusks. That night, I washed in warm water and realised I hadn't done that in ages. We were given a meal. There was chicken and pumpkin and rice to eat and sweet *vetkoek*. People were talking and talking and I wasn't listening, just eating. I was stuffed. The bed was like heaven – sponge and sheets and a real pillow. I slept like I was dead.

Next morning, I was still hungry. People shook my hand and introduced themselves. They were mostly from the same family. I wandered round waiting for breakfast while Zimry visited friends. At lunchtime, nobody ate either or offered me anything. Zimry introduced me to a woman named Koang who was a bit like my Ma.

'Are you ready to dance?' she asked. I remembered Zimry telling me I must learn and her question made me anxious. What was he telling them?

'I can't,' I said and she smiled.

'Tonight we will do the Dance of Blood. I'll teach you.'

It sounded horrible. Dance of Blood? Was I going to be murdered or something? I was really worried and went looking for Zimry and asked him about the dance. What he said didn't help.

'You have to remember two things,' he said. 'Dying is not death and your heart and the world are one. It's also not a good idea to eat anything today.'

Then he went off with someone else so I couldn't ask any more questions. I wasn't feeling good and his answers just made it worse. What had dancing to do with dying or my heart? I hated him shutting off like that. Really, if I think about it, I was scared of making a fool of myself in front of these people.

As it got dark, Koang lit a fire in an open area near the houses then walked back to her house. I was standing there with nothing better to do when some of the village women walked up. They had almost no clothes on, just leather skirts and a little apron of beads in front. They talked and laughed for a bit then began clapping and singing. It was beautiful but strange. One of them walked across to me and I realised it was Koang. What a difference from a moment ago. She had a short animal-skin skirt, beads round her chest, some rattles on her ankles and not much else. She took my hand and led me towards the fire. She did a little movement with her feet and waited for me to do the same. I went *step step* and all the women giggled. She said: 'Don't walk over the sand. Push your feet through it – *push push stamp*'.

More women came up and started going *push push stamp, push push stamp*. When I tried, Koang clapped her hands and said: 'Oooh, the problem is shoes. You must take them off.' She was right about that. Soon we were all going round the fire. After a while the women sat down, clapping and singing a crying song, high like birds. More women came, dressed the same, until there was a ring round the fire. They made a place for me and I sat with them, clapping but not singing because I couldn't do the clicks. At the edge of the light I could hear men talking. One walked to the circle and *push stamped* his way slowly round behind our backs. Then more men started and I realised one was Zimry. That was a shock. No khaki shirt. No baggy pants. He was bare except he had a little flap of leather like the others had. He was also shuffling and stamping. All the men went round and round like that while the women clapped. It felt really good to be in the circle and I felt dreamy, clapping and watching the men circle, circle.

Suddenly, one of them fell over. He bent double and rolled. A woman got up and stroked him and rubbed him with what looked like oil. I thought he'd had a heart attack but they didn't seem to worry. As Zimry went behind me he caught my arm and pulled me standing and into the trough the men had been making with their feet. I was in the line and had to *push*

push stamp or the men would have walked right over me. After a few rounds I was doing it just like the men, but it was hard to bend forward like that. We went round and round and I was getting really tired, but there was no way I could stop. Round and round and round. Another man fell and a woman went to look after him. I don't know how I lasted. We danced all night. My head was strange, like there was a big hollow space inside it, but my back and legs were sore. We danced until the sun came up. Then, suddenly, everyone just stopped and walked away. I didn't know where Zimry had got to and I was exhausted. Koang took me to my bed and I crashed. I slept the whole day.

When I woke up, I was still dizzy and felt nauseous. Koang gave me a few drops of something in water and the sick went away, but not the hunger. She soon sorted that out with a plate of porridge with a blob of butter and some sliced pears on top, all covered in honey. It was like a late afternoon breakfast. I ate really slowly, enjoying every mouthful. All the time Koang talked and greeted people who came in and out and asked me how I was feeling. Even though she was like my Ma she was different, because she was always happy, not stressed out. She worried about how few clothes I had packed – just a pair of shorts and a T-shirt – so she dug in a cupboard and came out with some things she said were her son's who was away in the city and wearing different clothes these days. She gave me four T-shirts and a warm sweatshirt and a cool pair of pants that fitted.

I was full and in my new clothes and feeling good when Zimry walked in. He didn't look happy. The first thing he said was:

'Why didn't you come across?'

'I didn't know where you were staying and I've just woken up,' I said.

But he looked fierce and said: 'That's not what I mean. Last night, you didn't cross to the Other Side. They were waiting for you.'

Hey, I was really confused. I asked him what he meant. What Other Side? He looked at me hard for too long to feel comfortable, then said: 'You know what I mean, Ky. I told you about the Other Side. I said it's the other side of death. Well, you don't have to be dead to go there. You go there in trance when you dance. The Dance of Blood last night was for you but you didn't come across. Why not?'

'I *don't* know what you mean,' I shouted. 'You tell me nothing. You don't teach me anything and you expect me to know everything. You don't even tell me what your silly Dance of Blood is about then you yell at me for not knowing what to do. Fuck it. Fuck everything here. This stuff is nothing to do with me.'

I ran out Koang's house and up onto the koppie behind the village. I sat on a rock just steaming. I was thinking that I didn't ask for this. I didn't even know who Zimry was, though everyone in the village treated him like he was important. I badly wanted to go home. And I wanted to see Auri. She might have had a way of making sense out of all this. I decided to go back. Stuff Akker and his Tough Livings. I'd cope with that when I got there. There was a road near the village, cars must come there sometimes and I could get a lift. It was dark when I walked back. Koang welcomed me like nothing had happened and asked me lots of questions about Cape Town. She had been there once and said it scared her. She said the plants were all wrong in cities and she heard they built roads over sacred places. I couldn't help her there. I mean, how do you know what's a sacred place?

I told her about Akker and gangs and school and my Ma and Auri and my time with Zimry. Everything. We drank rooibos and ate rusks and talked until it was late. Every now and then she lit a candle from the old one and her face looked nice in the light with her wrinkles and big smile with only a few teeth missing. All the time, though, I was being angry with Zimry. Eventually I asked her: 'Who is Zimry really?' Koang sat back in her chair. Then she sighed and said: 'How can I describe Zimry?

'He was born in these mountains, over at Wupperthal. When he was very young he got sick and his parents thought he was going to die. The doctor at Wupperthal couldn't cure him so they took him to a *!gixa* named Koerikei. He was of our people, the /Xam, and was a shaman with great power. He said Zimry had the Sickness of Sight and that the only way he could get better was to become a pupil to Koerikei. So he was trained in the *!gixa* ways and never went to school. Zimry has the *!Khwe* of *!khwa*. That means the potency of rain. He's a cloud rider and can make them go where he wishes. He's not a Healer like me,' she said, 'but he still knows a lot about the plants of this area.

'When Koerikei died, Zimry didn't stay in his village. He joined the Parks and became a ranger. But because he couldn't write, he didn't go far. It was apartheid days anyway. So he wasn't ever going to be anybody. I think he had an argument with the boss one day and decided he didn't want to stay down at Clanwilliam or Algeria. So he took the job of field ranger and went to live all alone up in the mountains.'

Koang was quiet while I was thinking about this, then she said: 'That is only part of the story. He is also the most powerful *!gixa* of the /Xam people.'

'Who are these /Xam people?' I asked.

She clapped her hands and said: 'Too many questions, Ky. It's time to sleep.' Then she gave me a candle for my room and told me to be careful because the roof was thatch. When I got into bed I wasn't angry with Zimry any more.

Very early next morning Zimry came into the room before I was out of bed to say he was leaving and that I was staying with Koang. I told him I was sorry I'd disappointed him but he stopped me by holding up his hand.

'I'm not cross with you,' he said. 'There are things you need to learn from Koang that I can't teach you. In a while, I'll come fetch you. I'm sure you won't object to some home comforts for a while.' Then he said goodbye and was gone. I lay there, my mind spinning. Was he really not cross? Had I let him down and now he was dumping me here? Would Koang mind suddenly having me in her house? Then I remembered my thoughts up on the koppie and realised the longer I stayed in the village the more likely I could get a lift to Cape Town. Also, I liked being around Koang. So I went back to sleep.

When I got up, Koang gave me some breakfast. I was embarrassed and she saw that. Koang saw lots of thing other people didn't. 'Don't feel bad about staying here,' she said. 'I'm really happy about it because all my children have gone away. So, for a little bit, you'll be my son. And we have lots to do.'

I asked her what that was and Koang went: 'Hmm, Zimry doesn't talk much. You and me, we're going to find out about plants.' And right there my lessons began. She went outside and came back with a bit of bush.

'What's this look like?' she demanded.

'We used it to make smoke in a cave. Zimry told me it's called buchu.'

'That's right. This plant's a whole chemist shop and it's been our friend for thousands of years. If you dry the leaves and crush them into fat and rub it on yourself, mosquitoes or flies will never bother you. That's good because flies are spies. Also, when there were lions, our people would rub it on their skin and could walk right past them and the lions wouldn't chase them. Maybe you have a sore stomach? You chew the leaves and it's gone. If you put some leaves in brandy it's even better for your stomach. Boiled up it can clean wounds. If you have a disease in your kidneys, buchu heals it. Perhaps your wee stings? It's a bladder infection and buchu's the answer. If you burn it, you call the spirits of the Old Ones. And as you know, it's good to smoke out bad spirits. Come, let's go for a walk.'

We had fun that day. Koang knew so much. We went up in the hill and she picked some green fruit of a plant that was crawling over the ground. 'These are sour figs. They're sweet-sour when you suck them. Try.'

I put the whole thing in my mouth and crunched. It tasted terrible so I spat it out. Koang clapped and laughed.

'No, don't eat the whole thing, just suck out the middle.'

She was right, it did taste good.

'This is *bietou*,' she went on. 'In spring it has yellow flowers, but now there are little grapes you can eat. Over there, that's *platdoring*, which can cure sex diseases and sore skin and stops people from having fits.'

That day we found hairy green fruit that cured headaches and coughs, tortoise berries that tasted great. I ate them until I was stuffed. I helped her collect *kattekruie* which she said she used to cure fever and sore joints and was good for people who couldn't sleep.

'This one's dangerous,' she said, 'so we need to dig it out carefully. It's called *gifbol*, but if you know how to use it, it can teach you to fly like a swallow.'

We were walking back to the house when a mantis landed on my shoulder. 'Aah!' said Koang, 'a messenger. I wonder what it's telling you.' I looked down and saw it had a grasshopper in its claw. It sat on me until the village, then flew off. 'I wonder what it was telling you with the grasshopper?' said Koang. 'I hope nothing's happened.'

Back at the house I helped her cut and mix the herbs we'd collected. There was a little room which had shelves of bottles and dry things and that smelled strange. Each day that we went out collecting, Koang would say: 'This is called whatever and it does this and you must remember it.' And then she would come to a plant and ask me what it was and what it did. If I forgot, she'd say: 'I told you this yesterday. If you don't remember these things you could kill someone.' Then we'd laugh. She wasn't fierce like Zimry.

Koang made me work hard, though. She gave me a notebook and a pen and I had to write down all the plants. I was walking and collecting in the early morning when it was cool, preparing herbs until lunchtime, then sitting with her while she talked to people who came for help. Koang had only reached standard one at school, but she was a doctor and people from the village and nearby farms came to see her for all sorts of problems. She would introduce me to them and say, 'This is my new assistant.' We'd listen to them and she'd ask me: 'What do you think the problem is and what would you suggest we give them?' like I was a doctor too. But if I got it wrong she never said anything in front of the people. She just said what she thought the problem was and she would send me to fetch the medicine she decided on. After a while I got pretty good. Often she agreed with what I suggested. I felt important.

I can't remember how long I stayed with Koang. It must have been many months – right through the rest of summer and the next winter. I learned so much and made good friends in the village. There was old Koboko who farmed pumpkins and potatoes, Duhu who sewed karosses out of dassie skins (I caught dassies for her and she made me my own kaross), Oulet who was so old nobody could remember a time when she wasn't there, but still she fetched water and dug in her garden. And then there was Fanzi, who was a bit older than me and looked after the sheep. We spent a long time talking about our different lives.

'A few years ago there was a terrible drought,' he told me. 'People nearly died of hunger. I think without Koang we would have. She found all sorts of strange things – roots, bark, bulbs – that we could eat.'

He also told me about his sister. 'She went to the city to find a job. She got a lift with a delivery van that came to Wupperthal. She said she would write and come visit but she didn't. We've never seen her again. It's been more than two years. My Ma and Pa are very worried.' I told him about the gangs and school, but I didn't tell him I was a member of one. I said nothing about Akker.

Except in the Blood Brothers I'd never fitted in anywhere, but in the village I was Koang's assistant and people were happy about that. I was just me and that was cool. Koang was like my Ma and a teacher and a friend, all rolled into one. I didn't know there could be people like that. I wanted to stay in the village forever. One day, a 4x4 came over the bumpy track where cars couldn't ride and I asked the driver where he was from. He said he had driven from Cape Town and was going back the next day. I could have asked for a lift but I didn't.

It was spring when Zimry came back. I was very glad to see him because I wanted to show him all the things I'd learned, but sad because he had come to fetch me. He gave me a big hug. We stayed a few days getting supplies, then we left early one morning. Koang said I could return anytime. 'I always need help with the herbs and you're good at doing them,' she added. She packed food for the journey. I couldn't look her in the face when we said goodbye because I would have gone all tearful. When we went over the koppie I got weepy anyway, but Zimry was walking a bit in front and didn't notice.

As we went down into our valley, Zimry's little hut looked terrible after the village houses. It seemed lonely and rough. And I was tired because I was carrying supplies and my kaross that Duhu had made. When I walked inside I realised there were no chairs. I'd forgotten about that. Why didn't Zimry have chairs? And my bed was hard after what I'd been sleeping on.

Zimry asked, 'Do you still remember how to catch dassies?' I told him I could do much better than that. Koang had taught me about what we could eat from the veld and I was keen to see what was in this valley. After a lumpy sleep on the mat I went out hunting early next morning. First I sharpened a stick, then emptied my bag so I could fill it with *veldkos*.

The valley was full of useful plants, probably because we weren't near a village and nobody had been looking here. I found *marog* leaves, which are like spinach and good if you boil them, *wituintjies* and *n/etjies* for roasting on the fire. And a whole lot of *veldkool* and *vinkel* roots which I dug out with my stick. There was *suring*, which tastes like vinegar and is good in stews. And, just to show Zimry I knew what I was doing, I got some *dawidjiewortel* which he uses for his blood and I even dug up a *gifbol*. Then I found some *koekemakranka* leaves that smell wonderful and with them I later changed the smell in the old hut. Zimry *was* impressed when I came back, I could see that. He said: '*Sjoe*, now you've become useful.'

That night, I made a stew out of the *marog* and *veldkool* and roasted the *wituintjies* and *n/etjies*. We ate until we couldn't any more and there was still some over. I was feeling really good, but I was still worried that I'd disappointed Zimry at the dance. I could feel there was 'something' between us that wasn't there before – you know how you feel those things? So I asked him what I did wrong that had made him cross with me.

'I didn't mean to seem angry,' he said. 'But I have to say I *was* puzzled. In the Cave of Hands you felt the power of the Other Side. Because you didn't know about these things, it was a bad fright for you. That's why I decided to go to the village and ask them to do the Dance of Blood. The dance was for you. But a few went through and you didn't. I don't know why and I can see you don't know why either.

'If you're training in the ways of the First People you have to know how to work with the Other Side. If you can't, then it's okay, but then you can't be a *!gixa*. Maybe you can become a Healer like Koang, which is why I asked her to train you. I see you're good at that. So maybe that's your path. But it's not something you need my help with. There's no need for you to stay with me to be that sort of Healer. I brought you back here so we can work this out together and make some plans.'

I felt like he'd dropped a house on me. I was still thinking like I was hiding from Akker and that Zimry was showing me things just because I was there. But I was realising he had a reason for me being there too. He was training me. And when that was over, or if I couldn't manage the training, he had no reason for letting me be with him. Like you can't stay in the same class forever. My mind was spinning round and round. I was a failure. It was a bad feeling, especially because there was nothing I could do about it. It's not like swotting for an exam. I went to bed depressed. I realised then that I suddenly wanted, very badly, to be a *!gixa,* and I was wanting that just when I couldn't be one.

The next few days I collected *veldkos* and cooked but the fun was gone. That feeling that something new might happen had all disappeared. I was missing Auri. Then I thought I'd be a failure there too because this stuff was important to her. That made me really desperate. I thought I could go back to Koang, but how could I spend my whole life in that little village? There was really nowhere to go. I sat in the cave and even thought about killing myself. If I ate enough of the *gifbol*, that would do it. Maybe it was a way to solve the problem. Then I thought about what that would do to my Ma and I didn't consider it any more. Why hadn't I gone to the Other Side in the dance? How could I answer that? I hadn't been scared or anything. I just didn't know.

I went to bed one night feeling all upside-down and anxious. First I couldn't sleep, then, when I did, I had a dream. What a strange dream!

I'm in the city, in Cape Town, and I'm watching where an accident has happened. A person has been hit by a car and they are being loaded into an ambulance. It's sort of hard to see things. Everything is in a blue mist. There's no colour. The accident is none of my business but somehow I'm in the ambulance. Then I'm the person in the accident. And I die.

Suddenly there's colour and I'm floating in space. On my left is the moon and it's huge, like I'm right near it. On my right is the whole ball of the earth, with blue seas, white clouds and green forests. It's beautiful. Between them is just blackness and millions of stars. While looking at all this, I realise there's a creature near me. That gives me a terrible fright. It has the upper body and head of a woman and the body of a lion, but what's really scary is that its feet are claws like an eagle.

With one arm it shows me the stars, with the other it points towards the earth. I make a choice and am suddenly in a line of people on earth. The row is so long that the people at the other end, down in the valley, are just little dots. There are all sorts and they're dressed in colourful clothes. They're all happy, dancing along the hill towards a young man who sits outside a little house. From him the line turns down the valley and the people at the front are going into a cliff.

When I get to the man, who is /Xam, I step out of the line and sit with him for a long time. He says his name is Xatten. I can't remember much of what we talk about, except that it's about life on earth and in the stars. Then I'm in the line again and soon get to the cliff wall. I see that people are going into a cave. When I step into it, I wake up.

I lay there being happy about the dream. It was big and real. Then I felt it was saying to me that the answer was in the Cave of Hands. I don't know why I decided that, but it was a strong feeling. As soon as I thought about it, the idea scared me. The dizziness and the rock pulling me in like that. But was it more terrible than going back to Bonteheuwel and Akker? The dream was right; I would have to go back there.

I told Zimry I was going hunting. I think he knew something was up. I walked all the way to the Cave of Hands. It was eerie to go in all alone because of the power I knew was there. I sat down and looked at the wall. The hands were beautiful. Some looked as though they'd been made by a person putting their palms in black paint. But others seemed to have been made by having white stuff sprayed around them. There were antelope and thin people with heads of buck and the person under the *kankerbos* who gave me such a fright the first time I saw it. Also, there were those rows of people you could see through.

Like before, the more I looked, the more I saw. There were very faint elephants that the rows of people had been painted over and some things that looked like monsters with big mouths but just blobs for bodies. Then I saw the red hand I'd touched before. It was, like, 'danger', you know? I sat there a long time just looking at it, feeling scared. It was worse than someone pointing a gun at you. Maybe they wouldn't pull the trigger. Maybe if they did, they'd miss. But I knew if I touched that hand, all hell would break loose.

A lot of strange things had happened to me and something even stranger was going to happen. I was a mixture of being depressed and excited, I can't explain. But worried also. I leaned over and put my hand on the red hand. What happened next is really hard to describe. Afterwards, I didn't know if it was the handprint that did it, or whether I went into a trance or what. I seemed to fall and it felt like I was stretching, stretching, with my feet in the cave and my head far away. I was flying forward, head first. All round me were sparkling lights like fireworks, zigzags and flying dots and light and then a curve like a rainbow right across where I was stretching. It felt like I was going to hit into it but I went right through. All the lights were throbbing, getting lighter and then brighter, then breaking up and starting again. There was a sound like crickets.

But then the light zigzags started becoming snakes and the dots had faces in them and the fuzzy light stuff was becoming things I couldn't recognise – really bad things, animals with their mouths open and big teeth. Also locusts everywhere. Zigzags became slicing knives and I saw bits of myself floating away. My arm was flying away and then the fingers of my other hand came off and became part of the zigzags. I screamed but there was no sound. Then all these things, the animals and the light bits and parts of me and everything, came together into a tube in front of me. It was as if I was flying down a tunnel made of nets of light. In the net I saw Norman and Cliffie. What were they doing there? Faster and faster. I was still stretching. Sometimes I seemed to be travelling under water. Then flying. I became a jackal. Then a fish. Then a leopard. I looked at my hands and they were paws with claws. I remember pushing the claws in and out, like a cat does, and thinking, 'How can a person do that?'

There were things all around that I can't describe. There are no words for those things. But somehow, after being cut up, it felt okay to be there and I was looking around and thinking, 'This is quite cool.' Then I saw something big ahead of me and I was flying towards it. It came closer and I realised it was

Akker. His mouth was wide open like he was going to swallow me. I couldn't believe he'd followed me like that. I was going to disappear right into him. I held my hands in front like I was holding a gun and yelled, 'Nooooooo!' Fire came out of my hands. Out the tips of my fingers. It wrapped all around him and he fell on his knees. He was screaming as the fire ate him up. Bits of his clothes were whirling above him. He became transparent and I went right through him.

I wasn't stretching any more, I was falling. Tumbling over and over and going down, not outwards. There was water below me and it was full of crocodiles. They were rising out of the water looking at me and snapping their mouths. Falling. Falling. My mind said to me: 'This is your death.' Suddenly I felt Zimry. Then I saw him reaching out to me. I knew it was Zimry but he looked amazing. Not the old man with peppercorn hair and a khaki uniform, but big and with clothes made out of light and colour that was changing all the time. He was flying after me, not tumbling. He caught my hand and swung me back over his shoulder and upwards. I could hear sounds like the *whoosh* of air going fast and we were flying together, with him holding me by the back of my neck.

We dived into a cool darkness and came up out of a spring that Zimry later told me was a waterpit. I flew up, but was sucked downwards and dived through the entrance of the Cave of Hands and back into my ordinary body. Just before I went into myself I saw my body sitting there with its head against the rock wall like I was leaning on it. Blood was dripping out of my nose. My body jerked as I went in and fell on its back.

I was in the ordinary world again. I felt as though I'd been run over. My face seemed to have mud on it and, when I brushed it, dried blood came off in my hand. I was cold, shaking. I lay there trying to figure out if that was all real or a dream or the sort of trance Zimry expected me to go into round the fire.

It took me ages to walk back. I was tired. I needed to wash. I stank of sweat and there was blood all over. I spent a long time drinking at the river, then washing myself all over. I let the sun dry me and walked up the valley to the hut. Zimry was on his rock smoking. He looked old and tired. I thought maybe he'd been doing his plant counts far away. I don't know why, but I hoped he wouldn't see that there was anything different. I thought he would call me stupid if I told him what had happened. But he said, very softly, when I walked up: 'Sit down.' Then I knew that he knew. I slumped down next to him and started to cry. He held me close against him and we sat like that for a while. Then he said: 'Ky, I wasn't sure about your abilities. I see now you're not a Healer. You are a Keeper. A Rainmaker. That's why you didn't go into trance at the dance. Only a Keeper can work without the dance. But you need to realise that you're on the path of becoming a *!gixa*. If you don't, it'll be very dangerous for you.

'Keepers are different to Healers. People call them Rainmakers because that's what they do. They have greater power and they can trance without dancing. That's how they can ride clouds and work with wind and rain. But you're too young to go alone into those places. Next time we work together, yes?'

I found out later that when he realised I'd gone to the Cave of Hands he wanted to come after me. But it was too late for him to catch up with me there, so he'd used some of the *gifbol* to go into trance. He'd caught up with me as I started falling. He'd saved my life. But *gifbol* is not good stuff. It's poison, really, and taking it had drained him. For the next week he mostly lay around while I hunted and fetched water and cooked. It was a strange time because my spirit was thin. I also felt drained.

Zimry and me were roasting food round a fire outside the hut, as we did each evening now that it was winter, listening to the sounds of the night. Frogs were shouting *ping, ping* down at the river and a nightjar was calling what sounded like *Good Lord Deliver Us*. He stared into the flames for a while. 'I'm a Keeper of Rain and so was my teacher, Koerikei,' he said. 'But he's dead now and I've never met another one. Even among the Ju/hoansi and the Nharo or the G/wi of the Kalahari in Namibia and Botswana or the San of the Drakensberg. There are none. I'm the only one left. I should have known that the spirits would send me a Keeper to train. I never thought…. I'm sorry to have judged you wrongly.'

I laughed because he looked sad when he said that, and it made him laugh also. 'How come Keepers can trance without the dance?' I asked.

'It's to do with eland blood. The reason so many eland are painted in the caves is because their blood is the doorway. That's why they were the sacred animal of the /Xam and why /Kaggen, who made the first eland, loved them. If the sun steals the power of the blood and the paintings fade, they won't work. If you have badness in your heart or are just fooling around and touch an eland blood painting, you can stick to the rock until you die. That's what I thought had happened to you when Steve was here.' Then he told me the full story about the birth of the eland that I'd dreamed about.

One day, /Kaggen stole the shoe of /Kwammang-a, who was the husband of his adopted daughter, Porcupine, and of the Pawed People. He took it to the waterpit where Rain lived, which is the skin between this world and the other. There he turned the shoe into a young eland. Each day, /Kaggen would tell his family that he was out hunting for honey. But when he found the honey he would feed it to Eland, which grew and grew. It was so beautiful that it made /Kaggen cry. In three days it was so big the ground shook when it walked.

But in the meantime, /Kaggen's family was angry that he brought home no honey. /Kwammang-a told his son, /Ni, the Mongoose, to follow /Kaggen and he saw Eland. He ran to his friends the Meerkats and when his grandfather went from the waterpit, Mongoose and the Meerkats killed Eland and cut it up to eat. They did this to get its power. When /Kaggen discovered this he cried. He was heartbroken. But when he tried to shoot the Meerkats and Mongoose, the arrows came back at him, because they had the n!ao *of the eland. The Meerkats and Mongoose beat the old man with his own knobkerrie.*

When it got dark, /Kaggen went towards the place where Eland had been killed. He couldn't see, so he threw his shoe into the sky where it became Moon. By its light he gathered up the blood of Eland that was on the ground and carried it to the waterpit, which is the doorway to the Other Side. He used the blood to seal over the door to the Other Side, cutting off people of the Blue World, this world, from the place of their beginning. He was angry with the people for killing his favourite animal. That's why the only way to the spirit world is through the blood of Eland. It's a doorway where there's much danger and anger, so you have to be careful.

'Why do the things you tell me about the /Xam sound like children's stories?' I asked.

'Stories are things that float on the wind,' he said. 'The /Xam didn't have writing to hold them. But the most important truths are simple so they could be told over thousands of years without changing. Their stories are a way to tell people what to do. It's like the hands in the cave. They're from *!gixa* long dead, but their power lives on in their paintings, especially their hands. It's about not forgetting.'

'So the Cave of Hands is a doorway?'

'It's what we call a portal. Those zigzags and dots on the rock are what you saw in trance, yes? You felt you were stretching going in, and maybe you even felt you were becoming some animal? The wall's a map if you know how to read it. And a warning.'

'So what about the bucks' heads and the elephants and...'

Zimry held up his hand. 'It's better to see than to talk. Soon I'll show you.'

After about a week we went walking up the valley in the direction I came when I first arrived at the hut. It was winter's beginning and had been raining. The proteas were like a yellow sea, rippling in the wind, which was cold. We crossed over a ridge and down into another valley where the bush was thick and hard to push through. Zimry led me to one side of the valley and behind some trees where there was a big overhang. The rock wall was amazing. It was covered in eland, full of colour and not like most rock paintings that are just red or black. There were maybe thirty big eland, right across the cave.

'Come look from here,' Zimry said. 'You can see the whole painting better.' From there I could see there was a *!gixa* in a shining cloak, just like the one I'd seen Zimry wearing on the Other Side, but it was made of all the eland, flowing away down the cave. The person was big, much bigger than me. It was the most beautiful painting I'd ever seen.

'I call this *!gixa* Cave,' Zimry said. 'Look there in front of the *!gixa,* at these smaller paintings. You see how people are stretched very long with eland heads and horns? And these zigzags and dots and a net? I'm sure you recognise them now. Here's a crocodile, and it's connected to the people and the eland by this thin line.'

'What's the line?' I asked.

'It's the silver thread of life. Something you didn't know to hold onto. It's why you fell. The /Xam didn't paint these things for fun. They painted them to teach others. Now you've been in a trance you can see how important they are.'

That's when I understood properly that the rock paintings had power. 'I want to find more of them and go back to the ones Steve and I found,' I said. Zimry grinned. 'I see you're learning to read. We'll be doing that.'

And so my training began and mostly it was written on rock walls. Zimry knew many caves and overhangs – I wondered why he hadn't shown them to me before, or to Steve. 'These are classrooms of the /Xam,' he said. 'They aren't art museums. They don't work anywhere else. They're like keys to unlock this rock or cave in this place. The business of the pictures is here, for you, now.'

What he showed me, in all those paintings, was like a book of instructions: do this in that way for this to happen. There were pictures of dances that weren't around a fire but circling a person who was being healed. Arrows showed where the pain was and how to take it out. There was one painting that had stretched dancers following a *!gixa* who was taking the sickness and throwing it away. Lots of pictures showed dots and zigzags and how they become the net and then the tunnel. There were the monsters you see on the Other Side. There was a picture of a *!gixa* but he looked like a guinea fowl with the head of a buck and long lines coming out behind him like he was flying. Another one, my favourite, was a *!gixa* running with long, thin legs full of squiggles. His body was like a standing-up buck but his head had horns and the pointy face of a jackal. A bird was riding on his head between the horns.

He was carrying a bow and had spears on his back. There was blood coming out his nose. Everywhere we saw eland, the guardians of the waterpits, and also the cracks in the rock and holes that *!giten* go into, which Zimry called portals.

Zimry was like a master standing at a whiteboard, pointing things out. But he was better than any teacher. All the time he was saying: 'We will see this. Then we will become like that. Then we will go here. These are dangerous and this is how we deal with them. These will help you, go with them. Always hold onto the silver thread.

'The most important thing to remember is the silver thread,' he kept telling me. 'It comes out the back of your neck. You have to reach round and bring it to the front. Then you hold it in a special way to travel with it. You can loop it to catch things, like cloud bulls and creatures. If you let it go, you're in big trouble because you need it to lead you back to your body. If you can't control it, you fall. If it breaks, you can't come back and your body dies.

'There are spirits that cause trouble because they've lost their threads. They try to steal one from people who travel on the Other Side. If they manage, they also steal your body.' I felt a shiver all over. How could something get inside my body? I thought maybe I was in the wrong place, that I shouldn't be doing this. Maybe it wasn't for me. I moved closer to Zimry because it made me feel safer.

Then, one day, he took me to what he called the Cave of Making, high on the side of a mountain facing the setting sun. There were huge elephants and rain animals and antelope painted on the cave walls. Also there were many people dancing and flying. All over were hundreds of things that looked like swallows but they had people's heads. Everything was connected by lines that went through the men and birds and looped round the big animals. I knew those were threads. There was a painting of many people fighting lions that Zimry said were the spirits of bad *!giten*. One painting was a huge thing that looked like a hippo but was covered in dots. Hunters were dragging it out of a waterpit into the world to make rain. People, standing around all thin from hunger, were waiting for the thing to come out. A nice painting was four men holding a thread that was wrapped round a thing that was running behind them. They looked happy because they'd caught it.

'I didn't want to bring you here until you understood the lessons of all the other caves we went to,' he said. 'This is where *!giten* have made rain since the beginning of the Early People. It holds the *gi* power of the Keepers. Tomorrow we will make rain together.'

We left the hut early next morning without eating. I was glad Zimry was with me. Also, I knew a bit about what to expect. I was very excited.

'See those high feather clouds?' he said as we walked, 'They're cirrus. We call them bird clouds and they're not much use. Rain has a body. Its legs are rainwater falling on the ground. Its navel is the storm. Its hair is a cloud. Its breath is a gentle mist rolling over the plains. The best are female clouds. They are big, puffy, white ones. We call them rain cows. But they're like young girls, never predictable. We need to look for the big, low, grey clouds with full bellies that bring steady rain. Their footprints are many little dots on the sand. They're */quaggi*. Zebras. Because they run across the sky and make stripes with their rain legs.

'The worst are the crashing thunderstorms. They're male and their spoor is big holes in the sand. We may have to nudge them away because they can cause floods and drown people and animals. They also kill with lightning. Some clouds you can ride. Others you need to pull. But you can only tell what to do when you feel the cloud's *n!ao*.'

At the Cave of Making we rested for a bit. Then Zimry spent a while looking along the walls for something. He said he needed two places near each other where the red contact points were best. When he found them he called me and went through what I had to do. 'Trust the zigzags and dots. Feel for the silver thread behind your neck.' I nodded.

Zimry had told me to bring a beanie so the rock wouldn't hurt my head, which sounded strange, but he showed me how we would sit facing the rock and rest our heads against it, then put our hands on the red places. We both leaned against the wall and he said: 'Okay. Now.'

I touched the painting and began falling. Even though I knew it would happen, it still gave me a shock. I was stretching, going past jiggling lights. Maybe if you were watching you'd just think we had fainted. But we were really through that rock in another place. Don't ask me how. I looked round for Zimry. He was there, not stretched like I felt, but flying forwards with his arms out like wings. It wasn't the Zimry I knew though. He looked young and his eyes seemed to be on fire. He had a kaross with strange colours pulsing through it. He reached behind him and caught a thin silver thread behind his neck and brought it forward. It was so thin I hadn't noticed it. But it made me remember and I reached backwards. The thread was there but it felt thick, even though when I pulled it in front of me it looked thin like his. Our threads went out behind us as we were flying down the net tunnel with all the creatures in the spaces. When it opened out again, I could see shapes and also people. Suddenly, in front of me was Akker, but not big like before. I could see through him. He grabbed at my thread but Zimry just blew him aside and we flew past. I looked back but he wasn't following. It gave me a huge fright to see he was still there.

Zimry said to me – well, he didn't actually say it like I am saying it now but I just understood he was saying it – that we must change direction. I followed him and everything got brighter and brighter. Suddenly, we shot out of a waterhole near the river and into the air above the mountains. I nearly let go of the thread, it was such a shock to be flying like that. I could see the mountains all rippling and purple going far from our place and then we were high enough to see over them to the sea. It was wonderful. Could anyone below see me? I didn't know.

'They can't,' said Zimry, 'we're in spirit space.' His voice was right in the centre of my head like it was my own. I wondered what would happen if I let go of the thread and Zimry said: 'Don't!'

I practised flying a bit and then Zimry said playfully: 'Let's go find a cloud. There's a good one.' It was huge, with rain falling out underneath it. 'Watch what I do and then you try.' He flew towards the cloud and spiralled around it, his thread making a loop. 'You don't actually catch the cloud,' he said. 'You capture its energy and it can fight you.'

'Your turn,' he said. It took a while to get my thread into the cloud. When it looped I got what felt like an electric shock. Zimry shouted: 'Don't let go.'

I could feel the energy trying to escape but we both hung on and travelled over the mountains towing the storm. Zimry reversed his flight round the cloud. I followed, and it was free, but flashing and rumbling.

'We're going back. It'll be scary, but don't ever let go,' said Zimry. We flew towards the ground. I thought I was going to crash but we went through the surface of the waterhole and into the net darkness. There were zigzags flashing everywhere and I flew out from the rock and into my body. The force made me crash onto my back like I'd been knocked out. My heart was thumping like crazy. Then Zimry said, 'Ky, are you okay?' It was his real voice.

'I think so. My head hurts.'

He reached over and took my hand in his. We stayed like that for a long time. Slowly my mind let me know there was a sound you don't usually hear in caves, which are very quiet places. I lay there trying to think what it was. The drum of rain hammering down outside the cave mouth made me sit up.

It was afternoon when we came down the mountain because we had to wait for the rain to stop. It had been a big storm and there was water everywhere and in our shoes. I was too tired to ask any questions and Zimry looked worn out too. The river we'd walked over before was running hard and we had to take off our clothes to wade across. When we got back I lit the fire to warm us.

'You'll be a powerful *!gixa*, Ky,' said Zimry, looking at me across the fire. 'It takes years of practise to hold a cloud and you did it first time. I'm proud of you.'

I fussed with the fire because I felt my eyes getting blurry. No man had ever said he was proud of me. When I was young there was just my uncle around and he was a drunk. I was a nuisance to him. In the Blood Brothers nobody respected me unless I was pointing a gun and they didn't think good about me for that.

'A bad spirit tried to harm you when we were going in,' Zimry said. 'It reached for your thread. Do you know who it was?'

'It was Akker.'

'Akker?'

'The person I was hiding from who wanted to kill me.'

'That's strange,' Zimry said. 'It felt connected to you and it wasn't the spirit of one who is alive. Are you sure it was Akker?'

'Certain. I hope I don't have to meet him again.'

'I don't think you'll have a problem with him,' Zimry told me. 'Just use your *n!ao* to push him aside.'

'It's a pity it doesn't work like that on this side,' I said.

'It does. Did you meet him when you went in before?'

'When I first saw him I put my hands in front of me and my fingers shot fire. He became transparent and I went right through him.'

Zimry sucked against his teeth. 'Are you sure? The traditions say only /Kaggen can use fire on the Other Side – that's why he's also called /Kan doro, tinderbox owner. I've never heard of anyone else being able to use fire.'

'Well, it looked like fire. And Akker became like mist.'

One evening, we were sitting outside the hut looking at the stars and I asked: 'Who are the *!gixas*?' Zimry filled his pipe, paying a lot of attention to it for a while.

'In /Xam they are together called *!giten* and are almost all people from the Old Races. In English they'd be called shamans or wizards. They've learned to travel to the Other Side, but to be a Keeper means much more than that. You take on the tasks of your teacher, who has received them from their teacher, going back into the time of Beginning. These tasks are guarding and assisting the *n!ao* of places – we make them safe for life, healing hurt land, making rain, keeping the spirit clear and strong. There are Keepers of many things – rivers, mountains, forests and even under the sea. I'm Keeper of the Southern Sand World. I told you that when we first met. Remember?

'Once there were many more Keepers than there are today. But the killing of /Xam people and also the great herds have broken many Keeper traditions. Farmers keep us from sacred sites and, in cities, you can't hear the voice of the earth or speak to the spirit of waterpits covered under roads and buildings. There are now many places and creatures without Keepers and the threads of life are unravelling because of that. I don't know – we *!giten* don't know – how to stop the Great Unravelling.

'Our traditions talk of the coming of the one who in the /Xam tradition we call /Kaggen, the Keeper of All Directions. Someone with great *n!ao* power who will bring back the Old Ways and train many people to work on the Other Side. But that's just a tradition. A story. We don't know for sure whether it's true.

'The thing about *n!ao*,' Zimry said, 'is that it can grow or get smaller and even get hurt. Sickness can hurt your body and your *n!ao*, or maybe just one and not the other. The *!giten,* the ones who heal, go into trance to see where the problem is. If it's just with the body they can use herbs, but if it's a damaged *n!ao* they must use their own *n!ao* to try to heal the person.

'It's dangerous if a bad spirit steals the thread of another person. If you don't act fast they just die. A *!gixa* can fight with the spirit and force it to give up the thread. To do this he must continue until the spirit is too weak to hold a thread ever again. It's dangerous and sometimes the *!gixa* loses the fight and becomes sick or dies.'

'So what's different about Rainmakers?' I asked.

'Rainmakers can do the things that other *!giten* can't,' he said. 'But their real work is not just rain, it's also with bigger forces like the *n!ao* of the earth. It's difficult, because the *gi* of the earth's energy is huge. You can pull a cloud or maybe calm some waves without too much trouble. But the power of a mountain or a big storm or a wind that has been gathering *gi* as it travels from deep in the Atlantic Ocean or up from Antarctica is too dangerous to imagine. You can't control things like that. You have to nudge them.

'Have I told you why some paintings have people with animal heads?' he asked.

'No. Why?'

'It's the creature to which their *n!ao*'s connected. Their spirit animal. Some *!giten* work only with animals. They see that the herds are healthy. Help them to migrate to where rain has made the grass sweet. They tell hunters where to find herds when they need food. Or they work with plants or birds or fish. There are *!giten* who can become birds or pawed animals. They use the animals' skills to hunt or the birds' wings to travel.'

'I want to do that,' I said.

Zimry clicked his fingers and said: 'One step at a time.'

One night, we were at the fire when we heard a strange sound. It went *rrrr rrrr rrrr* like someone sawing.

'Leopard,' Zimry whispered. 'Don't move.'

The sounds got louder and I felt the hair on my neck lift. I could see something moving at the edge of the light and its eyes glowed yellow. It looked big. But as soon as I saw it I wasn't afraid any more. The leopard stood watching us for a few seconds, then turned and was gone.

'Very strange,' said Zimry. 'Leopards don't come to human fires.'

'Maybe it's my leopard,' I said. 'You know, the one I called.'

'Maybe,' said Zimry.

I started asking questions about the shape-changing *!giten*. How could they do that? What did it feel like? How do you come back from being a lion or leopard? Could we do it?

Zimry didn't like the idea. 'It's dangerous,' he said. 'If you became a leopard, maybe you'd wander too far and get shot by a farmer. And leopards stay alone in their own areas. If we just appear in another one's territory, it could kill us.'

Just like gangs, I thought.

Next night, the leopard came again. Then the next – for

five nights. It just walked into the firelight, then went away. I had a feeling that somehow I was calling it. Zimry became really worried. But I could feel its energy and it made me tingle all over. I don't know why, but I felt safe in its presence.

'It could be a bad *!gixa*,' he told me.

'Where from? And why would it come to us?'

'I'm not sure. If it's a bad *!gixa* it could mean trouble.'

'How would we fight it?'

'Only on the Other Side,' he said. 'It wouldn't help to shoot it or anything. Anyway, we don't have a gun.'

'Well, let's go to the Other Side and see. Surely it won't be too strong for both of us.'

It took a lot of convincing, but finally Zimry agreed to show me shape-changing. We had to prepare, though. It wasn't like going to a shop to fetch something. For three days we didn't eat. We could only drink water. Zimry said we had to be light. At first it felt horrible to be hungry and I was a bit shaky. But Zimry gave me some herbs called hoodia and my hunger went away. I just didn't think about eating after that. In those three days I could feel myself becoming different – empty, but not weak.

Late one afternoon we set off for the Cave of Hands. 'Bad *!giten* are people who've lost their thinking strings,' he said as we clambered over rocks and into the valley. 'All people become spirit when they die. My teacher used to say they were spirit clouds. He said if you called some old people's names after dark as if they're not dead, they could harm you because they didn't have thinking strings. In the old language these strings are called */khu/khuken*, the things they understand with, which are in their throats. They can shoot arrows of sickness into people. Living *!giten* can harm you another way, by attacking you as creatures. Or leading Pawed People to you when you're alone. Becoming a pawed creature is called *jum*.'

When we arrived at the cave, Zimry sat outside and

explained how to do it. 'After the net tunnel, there are many creatures because that's where their *n!ao* gathers,' he said. 'It's where their threads are clustered. We must find a leopard and loop our threads around it. We have to be gentle otherwise it could think we're attacking it. We should make it clear in our minds that we want to borrow its body for a little while or the leopard might refuse. Because the human *n!ao* is so strong, we can take a leopard from the Other Side through the rock into our world. We leave its spirit *n!ao* in our sleeping bodies.'

That sounded complicated, but I wanted to try. I needed to meet the one who was visiting us. When we went into the cave it was getting dark. Zimry checked the paintings then found what he was looking for – a red lion painted quite high up at the back of the cave.

'We will both have to touch it as there's only one,' he said. 'But I think it'll work for us.'

We placed our heads against the rock and reached up to the lion. It took us through the rock and we soon passed the net tunnel. Zimry was moving round with his thread in the dark Place of Creatures and I followed. 'Here's one,' he said in my mind. 'And over there another. Use your thread to encircle that one and I'll do it with this one. I watched him flip a loop around a leopard that was also mist energy and transparent. I did the same with mine and I pulled it towards me. I felt the shock of its *n!ao* at being caught. But I made my feelings gentle and loving and it calmed down. I heard Zimry's voice say: 'Speak. It understands you.'

'I greet you,' I thought and a purring voice entered my head:

'Who are you that speaks?'

'I am Ky Rahl. A *!gixa* of rain.'

'What is it you wish of me, Ky Rahl?' the leopard asked.

'I wish to borrow your body for one night to experience leopard.'

'I have no wish to borrow yours.'

That confused me. Zimry's voice entered my head: 'Ask if it would sleep in your body in the cave while you use its body to travel. Tell it you will take great care of its body, if it will care for yours.'

I wasn't sure if the leopard heard that but I repeated Zimry's words. 'That's an interesting request,' it replied. 'Your spirit feels good and I agree. But I'll need my body before dawn. I can't trust you to hide it in the glare of the sun where there is great danger.'

'Thank you,' I said. 'I'll return before light.'

I wasn't sure what happened next and looked to where Zimry had been, but he wasn't there. I got a shock and called: 'Zimry!'

'Don't shout,' he said, 'I am right next to you.' I looked round and there was a huge leopard beside me. I flattened my ears and the hair stood up along my back. I crouched down and flashed my tail.

'You look just fine, but you don't have to react to me like that.' I could hear laughter in Zimry's voice. 'You're a very fine leopard.'

I sat down and pushed my whiskers forward, waggling them. Then I looked down at my hands and they were paws. I extended my nails and inspected them. I had *claws*! I stretched, pushing my paws out in front, and felt the ripple of muscles along my body. Old memories came into my mind. They were shadows of a world where I'd hunted and killed, where I was free and wild with soft earth underneath and stars overhead. I pushed my nose into some moss and understood the smells and where a mouse had walked. The energy in my body made me want to leap into the air.

'Let's go,' said Zimry.

'What about our thread?' I asked. 'I can't hold it with paws.'

'Don't worry. You're not on the Other Side now.'

Instead, we were in some thick bush. The sun was setting and we sat on a rock, watching it go. How can I describe being a leopard? My hearing was like listening on headphones with the volume turned up, but clear. When I heard a sound I could turn my ears towards it and cut out other noises so only it came in. There were smells I'd never imagined possible: plants, beetles, small animals that scuttled in the bushes. I could smell a snake that was not far away. I could also see the mist of things that had been there but were now gone. A buck had passed below us and my nose told me where it had moved and what kind it was. I even knew it was a big male and it made my tail twitch with excitement.

As the sun set, everything got a bit redder but the light didn't really fade. We stalked down into a valley and by the time we got to the river to drink it was probably night. An aardvark shuffled out of some bushes and a porcupine wandered along the river bank. I knew these animals only came out after dark but I could see them quite plainly. The aardvark looked right at us but she couldn't spot us standing there. I was so excited, I purred. The aardvark dived into a hole and the porcupine raised all its quills and put its head deep into a bush. Obviously they knew leopard sounds. Zimry chuckled and said: 'Remember the *rrrr rrrr* growl like sawing you heard at the fire? You just made it.'

Our paws made no sound as we walked over the side of a hill and down into another valley. It was like stepping on cotton wool. We nearly bumped into a klipspringer before it saw us. It whistled and leaped away. I was getting so used to seeing everything around me clearly that what happened next nearly made my blood stop. There was a hiss right in front of my face and something hit my nose hard. I leapt into the air making a yeowling sound and landed on my back with my claws out. My heart was going *wham, wham*. Zimry leapt to one side. He was snarling. Right in front of me was another leopard with one paw raised to hit me again. Her eyes were glittering with power and she made a low moan that meant trouble.

She didn't hit me again, though, and I jumped up. She did a surprising thing. She rolled over and tapped my shoulder without claws, flipped up and took a few steps away from me. She arched her back and bounced back towards me, tapped me again and ran. I couldn't resist. This time I chased her. We flashed through the fynbos while she did twists and turns, then she stopped and rolled again. I ran right into her and we crashed over and over, tapping and holding and pushing each other. It was fun. I took the role of leader and ran. She chased me, caught me on my back and tripped me. It was the best game I'd ever played. I felt the thrill of belonging and realised that for so much of my life I'd been living with fear: fear that my Ma would not come back at night. Fear at being teased because I looked different. Fear of being killed by gangsters. To my new leopard mind, human life seemed dull, slow and fearful – no smells, useless hearing, the danger of being alone in the world. As a leopard I seemed completely safe, as if I had enough power to take on anything. And somehow I understood – because my leopard survival depended on it – the way of trees and mountains and the living things around me.

Eventually Zimry's voice in my head said: 'Hey! Time to stop. Come.' My new friend and I were quite far from him and I didn't want to lose him so I stopped chasing and ran down the hill. The leopard thought this was more game and tackled me so we tumbled again. Each time I tried to run she pounced on me. I was getting desperate and cross. I snarled and hit her quite hard. She got the message and trotted next to me as I found my way to where Zimry was waiting. When I stopped she rubbed against me, purring.

'She thinks you're a good mate,' he said. 'She wants your kittens.'

'Very funny,' I growled. Then the three of us went further down the valley. All at the same time we smelled a buck. It was exciting to see how the leopard reacted. She got low to the ground and moved in little jerks, her eyes fixed on one spot. We followed without knowing what to do. She moved round bushes and flattened in the long grass without a single sound. It was hard to do the same. When Zimry stood on a stick that cracked she spun round and showed her teeth. We came to a clearing where the fynbos was low and saw a rhebuck standing grazing. The leopard looked back at us then went off at an angle.

'I think we shouldn't move,' Zimry said.

We saw only bits of her gliding between gaps in the grass. She was moving to where the buck was facing, then stopped and looked at us.

'She wants us to chase it towards her,' Zimry said.

'I'll go,' I said and sprang towards the buck. It didn't see me at first. When it did, it leapt forward and bounced towards my leopard. It saw her at the last minute and tried to jump over her. But she sprang up under it, catching it by the neck and then they both circled in the air almost in slow motion before they crashed into the grass. By the time I got there she had ripped out its throat. Her face was covered in blood and she was panting. Zimry came up and we watched while the leopard tore open the rhebuck's stomach and began eating the insides. She ignored us.

'Unless you want to chew some of that I think we should be leaving,' Zimry said. 'She looks hungry enough to eat the whole thing.' I ignored him and sank my teeth into the buck's shoulder. The blood tasted sweet. The leopard growled at my intrusion and I backed off. 'Come,' said Zimry and we walked away slowly with our ears back, listening to the crunch of the leopard's meal. Somehow she reminded me of Auri. I was sorry to leave her. We found our way back to the Cave of Hands and just walked past our bodies and right through the wall like it wasn't there. I went to where my thread was looped round the leopard and un-looped it. I suddenly felt cut off from my surroundings. The leopard yawned and stretched its body.

'Thank you,' I said. 'It is great being a leopard.'

'You're welcome,' said the leopard. 'Not very nice to be a human. Your senses are all asleep.'

Zimry and I followed our threads back out of the wall and into our bodies.

'What did your leopard say to you?' I asked Zimry.

'It said, "You're so boring".'

I suddenly felt tired and hungry. It was a long walk back to the hut that morning.

After sleeping deeply and long, I awoke early. White mist was swirling outside. I pulled my kaross over my ears and went to sleep again. That was when I had the dream.

I'm in a kaross all rolled up and afraid because I know there's a lion searching for me. I can hear voices, one of them being my Ma's. Then I'm picked up, put down again and the kaross is rolled so I spin round and round. I roll right out the kaross and before I know what is happening, the lion pounces on me and grabs the back of my neck. I can feel my spine breaking and I scream. The lion is dragging me away from the huts.

The lion lies down and begins to eat me. Each bit of me seems to be able to see and my bits watch as other bits are chewed and swallowed. Eventually we are all inside and I start to call all my pieces together again. While I do, the lion is roaring terribly, and when I'm finished it falls over dead. I hear people talking and then the lion is rolled over and over. I lie very still, not sure what's happening, and when everything is quiet again, I make my body grow until it's outside the lion.

I realise I'm rolled tightly in the kaross and I shout for the people to let me out. There's a lot of noise from the people and I hear my Ma say, 'It's Ky's voice.' I shout some more and someone unrolls the kaross and I jump up. The people are afraid when they see me and begin to throw stones, so I fly up into a tree. My mother comes and stands under the tree and says: 'The people do not yet know you are /Kaggen.'

I woke up and knew it was part of the dream that had saved my life – the dream that had brought me to Zimry. I told it to him and he smiled like the sun coming up. 'The dream is now complete,' he said. 'It's a story as old as time but you've never heard it until you dreamed it. It's one of the stories of the birth of /Kaggen. Hin Kabbo recognised your first dream. That's why he sent you here. He was right. Now you've completed the dream. I think you have a destiny. But it's not inevitable. Let me tell you something.

At the time white people came from over the sea in their ships and began killing the /Xam and other First People, there was a /gixa *of the /Kung people in the Drakensberg named Xatten. He visited the Place of Crocodiles on the Other Side. It was very dangerous. There, he was given a prophecy, which he painted on the wall of a cave. In that painting, First People are running, and behind them are men on horses with guns, killing them. People are on the ground dying. And there are wild animals dying. The men on the horses have hats like soldiers and there are saddles on the horses. Behind them is painted /Kaggen, with feelers like an insect, an eland head and a tail like Jackal. Behind him are many smaller pictures of himself.*

Xatten said the prophecy in the Place of Crocodiles was that the people of the Early Races would have to hide themselves and their secrets. They must never speak about the language and power of the rock art. These new people would not understand the Way and could damage the earth's n!ao. *The Old People would have to work together to save what they could. In a single moment they will have to travel to the Other*

Side and restore the n!ao *of the earth. It'll be dangerous work. But if they don't do it, most creatures of the earth could be killed by the actions of those without knowledge of the Way. The Time of Gathering will begin with the return of /Kaggen. That's the prophecy.*

About a month later, Fanzi came to say the fields were becoming brown and pear trees were dying because the winter rains hadn't visited the valley. It was good to see him and I showed him some of the caves. He was very jumpy about the Cave of Hands and wouldn't go in.

Zimry and I found a big, grey female cloud and opened its belly over the village. Before, moving clouds had seemed like a game. Now I saw how it could change peoples' lives. I wondered for how many thousands of years *!giten* had been working with the world to make it better for life without people knowing it.

I went back with Fanzi and spent some time helping Koang. It felt warm and sweet in her home. In the evenings we would talk for hours about all sorts of things. I asked her if she knew the prophecy about the return of /Kaggen and she did. That story was worrying me, like a stone in my shoe. At the village, I wrote to Auri to tell her I was missing her and asked her to come if she could. Also to my Ma to say I was okay.

I'd never written a letter before and it was strange putting down thoughts and feelings on the pieces of paper I tore out of an exercise book. I didn't know how long the letters would take, because only 4x4s could get to the village and the people didn't go out to the road often. And I didn't have money for stamps and hoped someone would stick some on for me. That got me thinking. I hadn't used money for over a year and I'd always had food and somewhere to stay. In the gang all we wanted was money. We called it *kroon*. We wanted to get rich by stealing and pointing guns. It seemed stupid. But that's how the city works – money and respect and power all go together. It seemed to me that money just causes trouble and makes people greedy or want to kill. Maybe Xatten's prophecy was right about the wrong *n!ao* in the world.

It took me most of a day to get back to Zimry's house and all the way I was thinking about /Kaggen. I'd seen the Place of Crocodiles and it was terrifying. But Xatten had found his prophecy there and, if I really was some part of the story, I could maybe discover some answers. Then I remembered that I'd met Xatten – in the dream about the Lion Woman. When I got back, I asked Zimry about the Place of Crocodiles, but he said nobody he knew of except Xatten had ever returned from there. It was forever death, spirit death, not the little death of travelling to the Other Side or even the death of dying.

A few months later, Auri and her Pa arrived. They just walked down the mountain like it was the most natural thing in the world, but carrying so much luggage they were panting when they got to the hut. Auri gave me a big, long hug that made me tingle and we walked down to the edge of the stream.

'Has it really been nearly a year?' I asked.

'Almost. It was December when I was last here and now it's November. I've just finished exams and *finished school*!' She shouted the last words.

'That's cool. How did you do?'

'Okay,' she said. 'But half the things they teach aren't useful. Except for science. It's all language and struggle history. Our people are just in the footnotes. What have you been up to?'

I told her about my time with Koang in the village. She listened to me with her beautiful eyes going wide and clapped her hands when she got excited.

'You've been learning more than I have,' she said. 'All that makes my exams sound easy.' I asked why she was here. 'I got your letter. And I have to start my training with Koang. But I told my Pa I wanted to come here first, then you and Zimry could take me to the village.'

'Your training?'

'Yes,' she said. 'I have to start becoming a */gixa*.'

I looked at her in amazement. 'You're going to be a */gixa*?'

'Yes, why not? Do you think only boys can do that? In /Xam tradition at least half the */gixas* are women – and they're some of the best.'

'I wasn't surprised because you're a girl,' I said. 'Just I thought you were so clever at school you'd go to university.'

'I could,' she said. 'Maybe I will sometime. But all my life I've been expecting to be a */gixa* before anything else. You know my Pa and Ma are part of the /Xam movement. There was never any doubt this was my path.'

'I just think… that's wonderful,' I said. I stood and pulled her up and held her tight. She took my face in her hands and kissed me. It was the sort of kiss you hope never stops.

'Will you help me with my training?' she asked. 'I'd love that.'

'Of course I will.'

We sat down and she took my hand.

'Ky, I've got something to tell you.' She looked worried. 'Norman and Cliffie were shot. They're dead. It was in a gang fight. I'm sorry to be the one who tells you.'

It was like my heart stopped right there.

'It's because of me. Was it Akker?

'No,' she said. 'It was a fight with the 28s. Ky, they were

always fighting. If you put a glass on the floor and throw a handful of raisins at it sooner or later one will go in. It's like that. They were taking so many chances and just fighting for nothing. And there's no more Akker.'

'What do you mean?' I demanded.

'He's also dead, burnt up.'

I stared at her. 'Burnt?' I remembered my fingers throwing fire.

'You remember those people who formed an anti-gang and drug organisation? While you've been away they became very strong. One night they surrounded his house chanting things like, 'Gangs out. Drugs out'. Akker wasn't home but he came when they were there. He was arrogant. He drove right through the crowd to his house and got out. Someone must have thrown petrol at him and lit it. He caught alight and died on his knees. It was all on television. It was sick. They showed it again and again. But it means you're safe now.

'But there's something else. I went to see your Ma. Actually, I went quite often. She is missing you like crazy. After Akker was killed I visited her and she was crying. I asked her what was the matter and she started talking about Akker. I didn't understand why. She told me that many years ago he was her boyfriend. She said he was very nice in those days and only afterwards he became bad. She told me he was your father.'

My mind went blank. I think it was trying to connect everything together but it was too much. I just sort of short-circuited.

'Ky? Are you all right?' asked Auri.

'I don't know,' I told her. My voice was shaky. Then I got up and walked up from the stream past the cave and into the mountain. She didn't follow. I went to a crack in the cliffs and climbed in. All the time I was thinking: 'I killed my father.' Then I was thinking: 'He was trying to kill me. And he knew I was his son.' It was all too much. I got deep into the crack and curled up and just went to sleep.

Auri's calling woke me. I was really confused about where I was and thought I was dreaming. But she kept calling and I answered. She found me there and lay next to me with her body against my back and her arms around me.

'I killed him,' I said.

'What do you mean? He was killed in Salt River and you were here.'

'I killed him on the Other Side. I threw fire. It wasn't petrol.'

'Yes, it was,' she said. 'It was in all the newspapers.'

'I killed him.'

'You believe what you want to believe,' she said. 'But let's go down now. My Pa wants to know what's going on. He'd like to talk to you and all you said was "hi" and ran off with me. Come on, get up.'

We went down and I greeted Mr Kabbo while Zimry made food for us. I was feeling empty and also angry. All those years Akker had known I was his son and he'd done nothing about it. My Ma was poor and he never helped her. I thought about all his money from drugs and protection rackets. Then I had the idea that maybe it was my fault. Perhaps he thought I looked like a Bushman and he didn't want to have a son like that. And inside all the anger and doubt was a sadness that said: 'I never knew him.'

'You heard about Akker?' said Mr Kabbo.

I nodded.

'Life works in strange ways, Ky,' he said. 'Zimry told me you met him on the Other Side and that you threw fire. That's a strange coincidence. The way of the */gixa* is to work with those coincidences but not to judge them. You'll never know whether it was your action that killed him or the result of the life he led. He chose his path and you chose yours. Why his life ended that way isn't a question you can answer. So un-ask it. He wasn't your fault or responsibility.'

I felt a great weight lifting. 'Thank you,' I said.

'You're welcome. Now, I believe you and Zimry are going to look after Auri for me? She's very precious. Please make sure she's safe while she's here.'

'I will, sir,' I said. 'She's very precious to me too.'

Mr Kabbo stayed for two days. On the second morning he asked if I could take him to the Cave of Making. Auri wanted to come but he said: 'I want to talk to Ky alone.'

Before, when people said that, it only meant trouble. But I felt safe with him. I also had questions I wanted to ask. At the cave he spent a while looking at the images. He confirmed that this was the main rainmaking cave in these mountains and he described the paintings in greater detail than Zimry. Down near the floor of the cave he showed me some crocodiles I hadn't seen – his eyes were sharp for outlines and colours.

'Where these are, is danger,' he said. 'But there are stories, old stories, that say they guard the root of the world.'

I told him I felt I had to go there, but he shook his head. 'It's bad, Ky. There are no guides for that place. The stories say that only /Kaggen can go to there.

'You were once angry about being called a *Boesman*. I think you've changed your views about that, though that word still pains me because it is not correct. Would you like to know about your people, the /Xam?'

I nodded and he found a comfortable rock. The story he told me, he said, had been handed down through far time.

'The place where the First People came out of the ground

and where /Kaggen made his eland was from caves to the east of here. Near Mossel Bay. From there they travelled to the north and west. Also into the dark forests. They learned the ways of the animals and the clouds because they were there at the beginning. They also gave everything its name.

'They lived in their way for many years and many generations. We can't count how far back in time. They spoke lots of languages and called themselves by different names, according to the families: G/wi, Nharo, !Ko in the Kalahari, !Kung in the Drakensberg and /Xam in the Cape. Later there were the Namaqua and the Khoekhoen and the Basters. They were all from the people of /Kaggen, the First Race. Are you following me?'

'I think so,' I said.

'When the Bantu people came from the north, the First People didn't fight them. They helped them find the waterpits and made rain when they needed it, because they were cattle people and cows are very thirsty. Not like the gemsbok. Still, today, the Xhosa do the Dance of Making, though they have forgotten the Dance of Blood. They made us their Healers and Rainmakers. They used our herbs and musical instruments. They even took our clicks into their language. Later, though, there was trouble and fighting. Many First People died.

'But it was when the whites came from over the sea that the terrible times began. There were fights about cattle and land and waterpits. The whites had guns and they shot animals without eating them. They often just took their skin and horns, leaving the flesh to rot.

'When the eland were gone, the *n!ao* of the /Xam became thin. This is because their power rests in the bones and blood and fat of the eland. Soon there was no food. In the Cape where the /Xam were, it was necessary to eat the cattle and sheep of the whites because there was nothing else left. Because of this, the Dutch and the English and later the Griquas said we were thieves. They got commandos and hunted /Xam in the mountains and shot whole families, even children. They called them Bushmen and Hottentots, which were not their proper names. Commandos cut off people's ears, and for these the government paid them rewards. Two rixdalers for two ears. But no rixdaler for one ear, in case its owner was still alive.'

'What about the pictures in the caves?' I asked.

'There were many great *!giten* among the First Races,' he said. 'They understood the ways of the sky and the world beneath the ground. To teach others and to mark the places of going in, they made paintings on cave walls. In the Kalahari they made them by chipping into rock. Some of those paintings are made with eland blood and are doorways, as you've found out.'

Mr Kabbo stopped and looked over the valley with great sadness in his face. 'For us the loss of the land is the loss of everything because it's the place where our minds live. So much was lost. So many.'

'Why is it that to call someone *Boesman* or *Hotnot* is so bad among the coloured people?' I asked. 'Why do I hate it?'

'It's a good question,' he said. 'I was coming to that. The whites who came to the Cape didn't like to work. Maybe they were weak. Maybe they were lazy. But they caught black people and some /Xam and made them slaves to do the labour. They even worked in the kitchens and one /Xam woman became the wife of Governor Van der Stel. But mostly they were on farms.

'About 200 years after the whites arrived, slavery was made illegal. White farmers were forced to let their slaves free. They were very angry about that. So they made a new law. Any /Xam person who was not working for a farmer could be caught and made to work for whoever caught him for 25 years. They were called *inboekselings*. The farmers would go on raids to the settlements of the /Xam and kill anyone who resisted. The rest were booked in as slaves. Even women and children.

'After a long time, the king in England heard about this. His government forced the Cape government to let the /Xam free. They had to change the *inboekseling* laws. When the /Xam heard about this they ran away from the farms. Thousands and thousands of them. But they couldn't go back to the places of their ancestors and their old waterpits, because white farmers had stolen the land. There wasn't any food for them to hunt. So they went to Cape Town. That's really where the coloured people came from. They are the /Xam and also the Khoikhoin.'

'You mean coloureds are really from the First People?' I asked. 'Then why is *Boesman* a swear word?'

'You see, there was a problem,' said Mr Kabbo. 'My people knew the farmers wouldn't be without free workers for long. They knew the *inboekseling* law would come back and catch them. So they did something very clever. They said they weren't Bushmen or Hottentots. They called themselves mixed race from white and black. Bushmen suddenly disappeared. If the white farmers wanted them they were gone.'

I thought this was the end of the story, but there was something he hadn't answered. 'Why is *Boesman* such a horrible word?' I repeated.

'Well, they were correct about the law,' he said. 'After a while it came back. But there were no Bushmen for it to catch, just maybe a few /Xam deep in the mountains. It was very dangerous if someone found out you were a Bushman. People learned to deny they were anything but coloured. They said they were mixed people, half black, half white. It was much better to be a bastard than a Bushman in those days, and even now. There was also the shame of being defeated. So if you wanted to do something really bad to someone of the First People, to curse them when there were other people around, you called them *Boesman* or *Hotnot*. People knew it was a curse but forgot why.

'This isn't the history you find in school history books,' Mr Kabbo said. 'It's things that people have told their children and they told *their* children. That's how I know. I am a Keeper of Stories.'

I can tell you, that made me think. That was when my head turned right around. When we came down I was looking at the mountains with new eyes. They were like the city of the /Xam. That night I went to bed and lay thinking about how I had got into so much trouble because of this mistake in history. That was the first time I understood in my heart that I was /Xam – and I was really excited about that. Also proud. I was from the First People, the magicians of Africa, the Healers, the Rainmakers. A Keeper. The /Xam were brilliant artists before the ancestors of white and black people knew what art was.

The next day, Mr Kabbo gathered his stuff into his backpack and got ready to leave. 'Take care, both of you,' he said to Auri and me.

'Yes, sir,' I said.

He shook Zimry's hand formally, hugged Auri and kissed her. He hiked up over the mountain and was gone. Auri stood watching until he was out of sight. It was good to see how they loved each other.

Mr Kabbo had left the tent and Auri fussed about inside it, making it neat and homely. In a few minutes she'd made it more comfortable than Zimry and I had managed in the hut since I arrived. It was wonderful to have a woman's energy around. It somehow made everything more orderly and easier.

'I'm not sure how long I'm going to be here,' Auri said after she'd finished. 'Pa wants me to learn the ways of the Dance of Blood and healing with Koang. I'm a bit scared of that.'

'Koang's wonderful,' I said, 'and you'll love the village.' We walked up to the edge of the cave and watched the sun turning golden as it sank. I told her about what I'd been doing. She was fascinated about our shape-changing.

'I'd love to be a leopard,' she said.

'You almost are one,' I told her.

Later that night, we were sitting in her tent and I told her I wanted to go to the Place of Crocodiles. 'I think I must go there,' I said, 'something Zimry calls destiny. Though he's never said I should go.'

'That's dangerous, isn't it?' she asked.

'It is.'

She squeezed my hand, saying: 'How can I help you?'

'I don't think you can. It's something I have to do alone.'

We were so much alike in strange ways. Before I'd finished saying something she would know what I was going to say and answered. When she spoke I knew almost before she did what she was thinking.

'You seem to be in one mind,' Zimry would say. 'Why bother to talk?'

Zimry spent a lot of time teaching Auri. 'You never taught me things like you're teaching her,' I said to him. 'I had to drag it out of you.'

'You were an awful pupil, Ky,' he said. 'So confused about who you were. And your anger was like a boil. I had to be patient until it got better. You never even believed you were a pupil. I had to wait until you realised that. Even now I don't know who's teaching who.'

'You're my teacher, Zimry,' I told him. 'There's no doubt about that.'

Auri and I would share our dreams. Zimry always wanted us to tell him as well. He spent lots of time talking to Auri about hers. I wished I could listen to what he told her but he shooed me out.

'Don't worry, Ky,' Auri laughed at me. 'I'll let you know what he says.'

One day, Auri asked me to show her the Cave of Making. I took some food and my kaross and we hiked up. She was fascinated by the paintings and ran from one to the next excitedly. I knew she'd love it. She was like a little animal leaping around squeaking with excitement. I sat and watched her – she was breathtaking.

I put my kaross on the floor of the cave and the water bottle and food on it. When she came and sat with me, I said: 'This is the Cave of Making, I wonder why it is called that?'

'Isn't it obvious?' Auri asked.

'It's not to me,' I said.

She stood and looked round the cave for a bit. Then she took off her clothes. All of them. She just dropped them, walked up to me and started undoing my shirt buttons. We stood there naked in the cave. Auri took my hand and led me to the kaross.

'What if…?' I said.

'Don't worry,' she answered, digging in her jeans pocket. 'We have protection.'

We did it, each for the first time, in the Cave of Making. Our *n!aos* arranged themselves so they fitted into each other. We knew that neither of us would ever be alone again. That day a single thing that had been in pieces was made whole.

Afterwards, we slept. When we woke up it was afternoon and we were hungry. We ate the bread and drank river water. Auri asked me which paintings were the keys to the Other Side. I showed her the red ones and she suddenly knelt down and placed her hand on one.

'Don't do that!' I shouted and she looked at me, startled, her hand on the portal.

'I had to see,' she said.

We heard the gunshot in the early evening. In those quiet mountains it was a shock. Pigeons flew up from the cliff face and lizards darted away. We were counting plants in one of the squares and Zimry looked up.

'Poachers,' he said. 'Or maybe farmers from outside the reserve. Perhaps they shot a buck. But more likely a leopard. They hate leopards because they sometimes eat sheep.' The shot had come from a few valleys away towards the Cave of Hands.

'I need to go there,' said Zimry.

'I'll come with you,' I said.

'They've got guns. It's not safe.'

'Then you need me to be with you.'

'Okay,' he said, 'but not Auri. I gave Hin my word to protect her.'

We began trotting in the direction of the shot, me behind. We heard another shot. As we came over a ridge we saw two men in the valley. Using some bushes as cover and crouching, we got close to them. They were bending over a leopard. *My friend* the leopard. I growled but Zimry put his hand on my arm and said:

'Stay here.'

He stepped out from behind the bush and said, all formal:

'You have no permission to hunt in a wilderness area. You will turn over your guns to me immediately.'

The men got a fright. One started to run but the other raised his rifle and fired. Zimry jerked backwards and fell. I couldn't believe it. They'd shot him. Blood spread over his shirt. The man lifted his rifle again and I dived down as a bullet smacked the rock above me. I scrambled up and ran low, like I'd learned to do in Bonteheuwel, dodging behind boulders and then through the valley behind the river trees. I was sobbing while I ran and heard the man crashing round behind me, swearing. The other one was shouting: 'Shoot him! Shoot!'

I circled round and did the only thing I could think of. I ran into the Cave of Hands and, without fasting or any preparation, I went right through the cave wall so fast I hit my head. I dived through the tunnel, not really thinking of any plan. Right in front of me as I came into the Place of Creatures was the leopard. She was terrified but I held her and stroked her and told her it was okay.

'I heard a bang,' she thought-said. 'My body was hurting. I fell and found myself here. What is this place?' She looked closer at me. 'But I know you.'

'Yes, you do. We played once. But now I need you to help me so I can help you. I need to go into your earth body. I need to be a leopard. I need your skin pattern so I can hide easily. Your fast movement. If you can give me your leopard body, you can rest in mine. You'll be a human, then we will change back again. Just for a short time.'

'I don't understand,' she said.

'I'll curl my thread around you now and then you will sleep for a bit. That's all.'

'I think my body is hurt. But you can do what you wish, my friend.'

I wrapped my thread round her and pulled back out the rock wall. There was a terrible pain in my chest as her wound became mine. I felt my breath coming short and fast. I focused all my attention on the pain and pushed it away until the hurt stopped. I opened my eyes slowly. I was lying on the grass where the men had carried me near their tent. One was sitting by a fire and the other was over near a tree. Their rifles were leaning against the tent. I sprang at the man by the fire and knocked him down with all my force. As he fell forwards I hooked my claws under his chin and ripped his throat. He landed with his face in the fire and I jumped back.

I landed between the man by the tree and his guns so he couldn't get them. His eyes were round in terror. I was about to spring again when he yanked up his jacket and pulled out a handgun. I recognised a nine-mill handgun and knew I was in trouble. As he raised it I heard a loud cry from Zimry's direction. I was about to spring sideways but the man's eyes went funny, sort of dead, and he sat down. The gun fell out of his hands.

I sped to where Zimry was. He was on his back and my whiskers could feel a slight breath. But his *n!ao* was going to the Other Side. My teacher and friend was dying. I roared. Then I ran to the Cave of Hands and dived over my body and through the wall. I untangled from the leopard and then didn't know what to do.

'It's okay,' said a voice. 'I'm here.' It was Zimry. 'Everyone has to come to this side. Now is my time.'

'No!' I shouted. 'No! I need you. I love you.' He wasn't holding his thread and I grabbed it. The one end just stopped like a cut piece of string.

'You healed the leopard,' he said, 'but you can't give back life when it's passed to the Other Side. It's not the way. Our bodies are just spirit shells. Our true being is here. And you have a destiny, I'm sure of that now. When you challenge the

Place of Crocodiles I will be with you. And there when you return. You *will* return. As Keeper of All Directions. You are /Kaggen and it has been my great honour to have been your teacher. Go now. And take great care of Auri. She is your life's partner.'

'Zimry I can't do anything without you. You can't leave me.'

'I'm not leaving you. I'll be even closer to you now. I will always be here beyond the wall. I am the protector of your *n!ao*.'

'I don't understand why the hunter didn't shoot me,' I said.

'I cut his thread.'

'You *what*?'

'I was here and I found his thread. I cut it. I bit it through. It was really tough and I was so angry he was about to kill you that I shouted as I bit.'

'I heard you.'

I was in an awful confusion. I didn't want to leave Zimry, but I wanted to get back to Auri. Then I realised there were bodies lying near the cave. Zimry read my thoughts.

'Leave everything. Even my body. It's nothing. There will be a search party and an investigation. You mustn't be around when that happens. Take all your things and go with Auri to Koang.'

What about the Place of Crocodiles?' I said.

'You will know when it's time. Go now.'

I held Zimry and he smiled. Then he turned me round and pushed me towards the portal. And I just knew not to turn around and not to call him back.

I don't remember how long it took me to walk back to the hut. I dragged my steps. I was very emotional. My mind was scrambled. How could I continue without Zimry? It was one thing to know he was on the Other Side, waiting. But what about his pipe? And his clothes. And his special spicy smell? Those were real, here things. I couldn't convince myself that his warm, earth body wouldn't ever be around again. He was such a big part of everything I had become. And how was I going to tell Auri? Or Koang? Or Mr Kabbo?

As I approached the hut, Auri ran up to me. 'Where's Zimry?' she demanded. Then she looked at me and knew. 'Oh no! What happened?'

'Poachers shot him. He's on the Other Side, but, but....'

'But what?'

'He's dead.'

'No Ky. He can't be! Oh it's not....'

She sat down suddenly and started to howl. It was more than crying. It was a scary animal sound that came from deep inside her. She covered her face with her hands and made the saddest noise I've ever heard. It just burst a dam inside me. I put my arms around her and sobbed until I could hardly breathe. We cried until we were weak and had no more tears. Then we just sat there and inside me I was trembling. But I knew we had to go.

'Auri, we have to leave this place,' I said at last. 'There'll be an investigation. People will come. We mustn't be caught up in that. With my background, I could get held as a suspect. Zimry said we must leave. Go to Koang.'

'I can't think,' she sniffed. 'I suppose you're right. It's going to be terrible when we tell the village. It's going to be awful for my Pa. Oh for everybody. He was so important to so many people's hopes. For their dreams.'

'I know. And for ours too.'

We packed our things that afternoon, careful to leave no trace of ourselves. Some of the things we couldn't carry we decided to hide deep in the cliffs. As the sun sank I made a fire and we sat staring into it.

'Auri, I have to go to the Place of Crocodiles,' I said. 'I have to honour the possibility that Zimry hoped for, Xatten's prophecy. He said he'd wait for me to go. But I don't know how to do that at the village. I have to do it here. In the Cave of Hands. Tomorrow morning.'

'But what if there's a search party,' she said. The cave is near where....'

'I have to take that chance. The cave is hard to find.'

'I'll wait for you in the cave.'

'No.'

'Well I can't wait here! This is where rangers will come when they find the bodies.'

'Yeah. You're right. Let's pack up and carry our things to the cave. Then travel to the village straight from there. But Auri, what if I don't come back?'

'You'll come back. I'll wait.'

We got up early and hid our stuff in the cliff. Then I dusted over our footprints around the hut with a branch, walking backwards with our packs, sweeping until we were on grass.

It was a hard walk to the cave, and I went a roundabout way. I didn't want to see dead bodies, especially not Zimry's. We pushed our packs and bundles into the back of the cave.

Auri kissed me and sat with her arm around my waist as I went through the wall. Zimry wasn't there but I could feel his presence. I felt love coming from him as pure energy.

I flew down the tunnel of lights. Maybe I had made the decision, but I was really scared. I went down, down until I saw them. A voice inside my head said: 'Go in the spirit of /Kaggen.'

I dived down, going faster and faster. The first crocodile reared up right in my path. I held out my hand and made fire and it disappeared. Then another was there. I made a circle of fire in front of me like I was painting. The crocodiles were just the beginning. Beneath them were other creatures, things with long necks, others with huge heads and rows of teeth. They seemed to be trying to stop me going down, but the circle of fire kept them back. I knew they were the creatures of ancient earth that lived before the coming of the great sky fire. They feared fire above all other things.

Suddenly I shot out of the place of darkness, like coming through the skin of the waterpit. But I was not in an ordinary sky. On my left was the great curve of the moon, so close I could see the round crater holes, and on my right was the ball of earth with swirls of clouds. Right in front of me was the Lion Woman showing me the way. I faced the place between the moon and earth and dived into the deep black of space.

Words made by people were never meant to describe what happened next, but I'll try. I must have been flying at a huge speed because stars were moving past me. But I wasn't 'me' in the way we normally understand. I wasn't going up or down but *out*. Getting bigger and bigger. Also there was no here or there. Everything was everything else, all connected. It's difficult to explain. I was dreaming it and it was real at the same time.

There were suns and planets, many with creatures on them.

They were strange, like we have never imagined. Some had great *n!ao,* powerful and much older than us on earth. Size changed. I looked at my fingers and they were sheets of stars. My arms and legs were columns of galaxies, with spaces of dark stuff between. I was able to look at myself and be me at the same time and *all* of it was my body. I watched, almost sleepy. I knew I could cause galaxies to collide or to collapse everything and start the universe all over again. There was no beginning or end. Just becoming and fading away. Almost like breathing.

It was pleasant to stay still. Time wasn't as we understand it on earth. I moved it a bit forward then backwards, making patterns change. Creatures lived and died and become other things. I watched planets that grew green and beautiful. Others that went brown with dust or were stolen by ice. I saw how easy it was for suns and planets and creatures to die. Always, somewhere, life gathered itself together and grew in ever more wonderful forms. My mind asked the question:

'What is life?' And I answered: 'All of it.'

I knew I could stay here, like this, forever. Then I thought of Auri waiting for me, trusting I would return. Her love drew me back. Down through glittering stars and great dark emptiness into the place we call the Milky Way. Down towards our sun and its blue treasure planet. I stopped when I could see the earth clearly. It was a glittering jewel in space. I made time run back and saw the planet covered in great forests. Then there was a time of fires and a flaming meteor crashed down, covering the earth in clouds.

I made time go forward and realised there were many futures, like fingers on my hand. I watched one future as forests once again spread. And all signs of humans disappeared. On another time thread cities got smaller. Great disks at the north and south poles fed sun energy to the world. I knew that for humans to survive I had to gather the people of the First Races who understood the way of *n!ao.* With them, I had to begin healing. Opening again the door to the Other Side. My job was to restore the balance of the world. It wasn't going to be easy.

I felt Auri calling me. I brought time to now and dived into the space between the moon and earth and through the dark place. Nothing tried to stop me coming back. Not the strange creatures nor the crocodiles, because I was glowing like fire. I came up and felt Zimry with me. His voice in my head said, 'You are the Keeper of All Directions. The prophecy has been fulfilled.'

I went through the wall and lay at last in my little planet in my tiny earth body in a cave of the Chameleon Mountains, which are the Cederberg. I lay there looking up at the cave roof, loving it, and reached up my hand to stroke it. I heard Auri close to my ear.

'Ky, you're glowing.' Her voice sounded all hushed. She touched my arm. 'How far did you go?'

'All the way, I think. But you brought me back.'

'I wish you wouldn't come through the wall so fast like that,' she said.

I was exhausted and lay there for a while with Auri curled up with her head on my shoulder. Finally, I remembered the urgency.

'We need to go, Auri. Though I feel I can't walk a step.'

We hauled our packs onto our backs and I picked up my kaross. Then we pushed round the bushes in front of the cave and right in front of us was a ranger. His mouth opened and he grabbed for his pistol on his hip. Then he stared past us, dropped his arm and walked away.

'Come, Auri. This way,' I whispered. We walked silently up the valley and over a ridge.

'What happened?' she asked when we stopped to catch our breath.

'I changed what he saw,' I said.

'You can do that?' She stared at me.

'I think I can do many things.'

'Well, just don't disappear from me.'

'I won't,' I laughed.

It was a long and tiring trip to the village. It took two days and we spent the night in an overhang huddled together in my kaross. Koang sat with tear-filled eyes when we talked about Zimry being on the Other Side. When I described the journey through the Place of Crocodiles she held a hand over her mouth and stared at me.

'Are you /Kaggen?'

'I've been given powers,' I said, 'and responsibilities. Who I am is something I'll need to discover. I think the Time of Gathering is close.'

Koang called the village together and got me to tell the story of the poachers and Zimry's death over again. But I said nothing about my journey to the Other Side. People wailed and it was hard to continue talking. Koang did a ceremony of farewell, burning herbs and leading the village in a song that rang through the valley. Voices rose and fell, some old and deep, others those of children. It began with slow sadness and rose higher and faster until it was pure joy. I felt the weight of my teacher's death lifting from my shoulders. Song is the voice of the spirit.

Auri began her training with Koang. Deep one night, as the women clapped, she learned to do the Dance of Blood. She became Koang's apprentice and there was little for me around the village. My need to return to the world was strong. One morning, Fanzi told me he was going to the city to look for his sister. He said he would walk to the road and get a lift with a delivery truck that travelled from Wupperthal each month.

'Do you want to come with me?' he asked.

'What do you think I should do?' I said to Auri that evening as we sat in Koang's warm *voorkamer* with its smell of herbs and cooking.

'What is your destiny?' she replied.

'But you...?'

'Koang says I'm learning fast and will be finished in nine months. Then I'll come. I'll miss you like crazy, but life can't part us for long. We're one. What about the gangs, though?'

'Akker's gone and I'm... different now. I think I'll start my work with them. I have powers they'll soon learn to respect if they threaten me. Then there's the Great Work. For that we need to be together.'

'Just be careful,' she said. 'You're very precious to me.'

'I will be.'

As Fanzi and I boarded the truck, the excitement of seeing my Ma made me almost shout with joy.

'Where do you want to be dropped off?' asked the driver.

'Bonteheuwel,' I said. 'It's my home.'

'Yo! You come from a tough neighbourhood.'

'Yes,' I said, looking at the sun sparkling on the yellow *sonbessies*, 'but a beautiful planet.'

He changed gears and the engine whined as we ground out of the steep valley.

Glossary

!giten (/Xam) shaman (plural)
!gixa (/Xam) shaman (singular)
!khwa (/Xam) rain
!khwe (/Xam) potency
/Kan doro (/Xam) tinderbox owner, another name for /Kaggen
/khu/khuken (/Xam) thinking strings, said to be situated in the throat
/Xam the southern San group of people in Africa
28s a prison gang. There are also 26s and 27s.
anteater *Orycteropus afer*, a nocturnal mammal that lives mainly on termites
babotie a traditional Cape Malay dish
bakkie (Afr) an open-backed truck
Basters a Hottentot clan of mixed race, later known as the Griquas
bietou *Chrysanthemoides mmoniliferia*, a shrub with yellow flowers and fleshy, edible red or black fruit
Boesman (Afr) Bushman
Boland (Afr) a highland area surrounding Cape Town; literally, 'higher land'

Bonteheuwel a poor township in Cape Town

bossiestroop a syrup prepared from the nectar of the common sugarbush, *Protea repens*

buchu *Agathosma betulina*, a bush with round leaves that give off a characteristic smell when crushed or burnt. Used in ceremonies or for healing

Cape Flats a sandy, low-lying area around the Cape Peninsula that was once a sea bed

Cederberg mountains to the north of Cape Town

Citrusdal a town on the Cederberg

dagga *Cannabis sativa*, a bush whose leaves have medicinal and hallucinatory qualities

Dance of Blood the trance dance of the /Xam and other San people

dassie a rock hyrax, *Procavia capensis*, a small mammal that lives socially in rock shelters

dawidjiewortel *Cissampelos capensis*, a climber plant whose roots have exceptional healing qualities

deurmekaar (Afr) mixed up

District Six a coloured residential area of Cape Town that was razed under apartheid

Drakensberg (Afr) a high range along the eastern edge of South Africa; literally 'Dragon Mountains'

frikkadels (Afr) meatballs

fynbos (Afr) the general name of the biome found in the Western Cape; literally, 'fine bush'. Also the name given to a vegetation type common in the biome

gi (/Xam) spirit energy

gifbol (Afr) a bulb, *Boophane disticha*, used as an arrow poison. Extremely dangerous. Minute quantities were used by shamans for trance purposes. Literally, 'poison ball'

Hottentot a Khoekhoen people of southern Africa. *Hotnot* is a derogatory version of this

inboekselings (Afr) the booked ones – under the Masters and

Servants Act in the mid-19th century, Bushmen could be 'booked' into servitude for 25 years

ja (Afr) yes

jakkalskos (Afr) *Hydnora africana*, a parasitic, leafless plant that grows on the roots of other plants. Fruits are bright red and edible, delicious when baked and can be used to make a type of ice cream. Literally, 'jackal food'

jum (/Xam) pawed, of the cat family

Juss (Afr) an expression of surprise, from 'Jesus'

kak (Afr) shit, used as an expression of something disagreeable

kankerbos (Afr) cancer bush, *Sutherlandia frutescens*, a shrub with a multitude of medicinal uses

Karoo a dry, semi-desert area that covers most of the interior of South Africa

kaross (/Xam) a cloak or blanket made from animal skins

kattekruie *Ballota africana*, a flowering shrub used for a wide range of ailments

Khoekhoen a pastoral people in southern Africa related to the /Xam

khwaka !gixa (/Xam) shaman of rain

klipspringer (Afr) *Oreotragus oreotragus*, a small, agile antelope; literally, 'rock jumper'

knobkerrie (Afr) stick with a knob at one end used for hunting or fighting

koekemakranka (/Xam) *Gethyllis afra*, a beautifully perfumed bulbous plant with edible fruit

kooigoed (Afr) *Helichrysum odoratissimum*, a perennial herb used as a ritual incense and as bedding material; literally, 'cow stuff'

kouterie *Sceletium tortuosum*, used as a local anaesthetic

kroon (Afr) money

lap (Afr) rag

Mandrax a barbituate drug generally crushed and smoked with dagga